ADAPTED BY BENJAMIN ZEPHANIAH AND RICHARD CONLON

FACE
THE PLAY

Activities by
Mike Royston

www.heinemann.co.uk

✓ Free online support
✓ Useful weblinks
✓ 24 hour online ordering

01865 888080

Heinemann is an imprint of Pearson Education Limited, a company incorporated in England and Wales, having its registered office at Edinburgh Gate, Harlow, Essex, CM20 2 JE. Registered company number: 872828

www.heinemann.co.uk

Heinemann is a registered trademark of Pearson Education Limited

Text © Richard Conlon and Benjamin Zephaniah 2008

This edition of *Face* first published 2008

Introduction by Richard Conlon ©

15
11

British Library Cataloguing in Publication Data is available from the British Library on request.

ISBN 978 0 435 233 440

Typeset by Phoenix Photosetting, Chatham, Kent
Original illustrations © Harcourt Education Limited 2008
Cover photograph by Michael Wildsmith
Printed in China (CTPS/ 11)

Acknowledgements
Every effort has been made to contact copyright holders of material reproduced in this book. Any omissions will be rectified in subsequent printings if notice is given to the publishers.

Contents

Introduction by Richard Conlon

Face is a story about what is on the surface and what is underneath. Of course it deals with the pain of disfigurement, but the real story is about what goes on in Martin's heart and mind. Martin is embarking on a journey, but we only see the first few steps. What Martin begins to realise as we leave him is that he should be judged not on his skin, but on his character. The lessons learned by Martin and those around him are universal. They have something valuable to say about attitudes to disabilities as well as colour and national prejudices.

It was a challenge and a pleasure to adapt the novel into a play. Trying to get a sense of the pace, liveliness and colour of Martin's part of town whilst also looking at the internal struggle of a single soul was not easy. I hope it gives readers and performers a range of performance styles to get their teeth into. I hope too that it raises debate; debate about what Martin might do next, about how his friends have treated him, about Natalie's choices and about Anthony's role in Martin's life. There's lots to talk about and lots to disagree on.

The age group this play is aimed at is a special one – one where we begin to become the adults we may be for a long time. The choices we make about how we engage with the world as young teenagers can affect us for years to come. I hope that in some small way, *Face* might help with some of those choices.

Richard Conlon

Cast list

Street Voices (6)
Present Martin
Past Martin
Narrative Martin
Matthew
Mark
Natalie
Mum
Dad
Anthony
Dr Owens
Nurse 1
Nurse 2
Form Tutor
Gym Teacher (Mr Hewitt)
Head Teacher
Marcia
Officer
Vikki
Pete Mosley
Apache
Pusher
Margaret
Simon
Reverend Sam
Young Man
Announcer
Photographer

Adaptor's notes

The nature of much of this stage adaptation (particularly Act One) is fairly fractured and some conventions and devices may seem surreal. I hope that in some way this reflects and articulates the nature of what trauma does to people. Something of us is somehow 'stuck' in any recent shocking episode and it takes time to process and make sense of the events that have led up to it. My aspiration is that a ruptured narrative structure, whilst presenting challenges in terms of performance and initial comprehension, gives more depth and substance than a simple unfolding of chronological events.

The part of Martin is played by three actors in this text: a **Past Martin** from *before* the crash (who is barely in Act Two), a **Present Martin** from *after* the event: both of these play two facets of the same person and are conventional, if split, characters. **Narrative Martin** is above and beyond the action of the play. He is what we all want to be, with the ability to voice inner feelings and opinions, freeze the action and comment on scenes – for the most part he talks directly and comfortably to the audience. Narrative Martin can range freely across the stage, going to where the action is, and taking the audience's attention with him. Having one character portrayed by three actors presents challenges – the actors playing Martin need to find patterns of speech and physicality that will assure the audience that they are three facets of the same person.

The **Street Voices** are a fluid device with many functions. They push the story along, describe spaces and atmospheres, and can also play smaller named characters as well as roles in school classrooms, clubs, streets, etc.

A number of parts (**Form Tutor, Nurse 1, Nurse 2, Dr Owens, Officer** and others), whilst sometimes being nominally male or female in Benjamin Zephaniah's book, are actually gender-neutral and can be read or acted by either sex.

Act One

Prologue

The three Martins walk on stage, face each other, look closely. They circle as they put up a hand to touch the skin on their faces, suddenly recoil. Their movements happen in perfect time with each other.

A sound montage builds: school voices, feet in corridors, school bell, car tyres screech, crash, broken glass, sirens, heart monitor. Then sudden silence.

NATALIE   Martin?

MARK   Martin?

MUM   Martin?

ALL MARTINS   *(turning to face the rest of the cast)* What?

All cast take a sharp intake of breath on seeing the face and turn away, except Mum and Dad.

DAD   Are you okay, son?   5

Past Martin walks off and takes up a carefree still-image with Mark and Matthew. Present Martin takes up a place on a hospital bed.

The Street Voices take up centre stage around Narrative Martin.

STREET VOICES   This is a street story. Urban, capital, Eastside.
1 & 2   No green fields, no cattle grazing, just trees in parks with benches and bins.

STREET VOICES 3 & 4	This is a story of grey cracked paving slabs and charcoal tarmac. Seasons of winter 10 pale-slate skies and summer sun heat-haze on burn-black tacky tar.
STREET VOICES 5 & 6	But there is colour here, in the people, the voices, the accents, the clothes, the smells, the tastes. 15
STREET VOICE 1	This place has an edge, a lust for life, a speed, a pace, a passion.
NARRATIVE MARTIN	This is the story of how I learned more when the final bell on the final lesson on the final day of term rang out, than I did in the 20 whole year before. It was a time like no other, something was lost, something was found. I changed – inside and out. I grew.
	Yeah … this is the story of how I went from the gang of three – to the gang of me. How 25 I went from that *(indicates the carefree image)* to that *(the hospital bed)* like that *(clicks his fingers)*.
	Look at us. Martin, Matthew and Mark – Mum called us –
MUM	'A bunch of saints.' 30
NARRATIVE MARTIN	But saints *we were not*. But we weren't devils either. Just lads. East London lads.

Scene 1

School bell. Noise from a classroom.

FORM TUTOR	*(calling to keep control)* Now just because the bell has gone, that does not mean *you* can.

PAST MARTIN	Oh come on!
FORM TUTOR	A quick word. Now everyone. Please. Use your holiday time constructively. Stay safe; 5 do not give this school a bad reputation or your parents nervous breakdowns! Remember the things we've been talking about in citizenship and particularly in Drug Awareness Week. 10
MARK	We're not *stupid*.
PAST MARTIN	I learned a lot in those sex lessons! I'll use that this holiday.
MATTHEW	You hope!
FORM TUTOR	And while you are out there having fun, 15 remember next term will be your last in this year. So now you should seriously begin to consider what type of employment or further education you will go on to. Don't *waste* this holiday period – talk to your parents, look 20 up your options and remember there is no reason why you shouldn't use some of your time to study.
MATTHEW	Study!?
FORM TUTOR	Yes, Matthew, *study*. 25
MARK	But if you have to think about *work* and *study* on holiday then it's not much of a holiday is it?
FORM TUTOR	Is that right, Mark?
PAST MARTIN	I've got nothing new to learn, my head's full. 30
FORM TUTOR	Education never ceases, Martin Turner – and we all have more to learn than we may think.

PAST MARTIN	*(dismissive)* Whatever…
FORM TUTOR	And perhaps you might like to get some *practice* in too, Martin. Too many late nights 35 and late mornings, too many burgers and chips and that place on the gymnastics team may slip through your fingers.
PAST MARTIN	No worries – I'm naturally fit, me. Eat what I like, drink what I like and it's always the 40 same, stay up as late as I like and I'm still bright and up for it next day. Still got the moves. I'm pretty fly for a white guy.
FORM TUTOR	Whatever that means. Now – go!

Form Tutor freezes and Narrative Martin takes a good close-up look.

NARRATIVE MARTIN	I still remember what you said, that day *of* 45 *all days*: 'we all have more to learn than we may think' … *(turns to the audience)* … I hate it when teachers are right.

A beat, then a sudden switch of attention to the hospital bed. Mum is agitated, Dad is quiet and still.

MUM	Look at him. Look at him!
DAD	I am looking at him. 50
NARRATIVE MARTIN	*(looking over, walking across)* She's got a point, my mum. Look at me.
MUM	That is my son. My only child!
DAD	Mine too, love. Mine too.
MUM	It's this area, that's what it is – it's terrible, I 55 knew we should have moved us all to Upminster long ago. You can't bring kids up

around our end without having to watch
them every minute of the day. The drugs, the
violence, the lack of respect.   60

DAD   This could happen anywhere.

MUM   But it didn't. It happened here – to him.
(a beat) You…

DAD   What?

MUM   You wanted to stay here. 'I'll miss my mates,'   65
you said. Your mates! Look at him now –
look at him now.

NARRATIVE MARTIN   I didn't know any of this was happening –
well out of it, I was. Best that way.

DAD   I know you want to blame this on someone,   70
love – but this wasn't me. I didn't do this.

MUM   It's this place! This dreadful place.

DAD   Come here. *(they embrace)*

NARRATIVE MARTIN   They did more of that after the accident –
more hugging, more holding hands. I   75
noticed that. Like they'd been reminded of
what was special, what should be … what's
the word…? 'Cherished.'

MUM   He was born here…

NARRATIVE MARTIN   *(surprised)* Oh yeah, I'd forgotten that!   80

MUM   I don't want him to… *(as if she is about to say
'die here')*

DAD   He won't love, he won't.

NARRATIVE MARTIN   Fifteen years. A long time for such a short
journey. Fifteen years to get me from there
to here, the maternity ward to – to the   85
burns unit.

MUM	He was so small, all naked and vulnerable and covered in blood.
NARRATIVE MARTIN	*(pointing at the bed)* And look at me now – some things never change. 90

Scene 2

STREET VOICE 1	There's a special magic in the air on a warm Friday, last day of term. A crackle of freedom and expectation. Everyone was out, but it was cool. All the gangs. So many gangs.
ALL STREET VOICES	Everyone needs to belong. 5
STREET VOICE 6	At the rec there was the Big E –
STREET VOICE 5	'E' meaning East, of course…
STREET VOICE 6	– and on the corner by the chip shop was the Punjabi Lions, they were mainly Sikhs. Then there was a gang called the Positive 10 Negatives – they were parading up and down, seeing and being seen.
STREET VOICE 3	But it was safe.
STREET VOICE 2	Muslim gangs, Chinese gangs. And the *Big Six Posse*, they were the most respected 15 and feared school gang in the whole of East Ham, big black guys, massive, real scary guys but on that evening even they were just out there massing it up.
STREET VOICE 4	Chilling. It was all good. 20
NARRATIVE MARTIN	Funny isn't it? You take a word like 'gang', and you've got *the fear*, there, right away. But you put in a word like 'band' or 'group' or 'family', and suddenly it doesn't seem so bad. And no one talks about 'a gang of 25

businessmen' or 'a gang of teachers', do they? Me and Mark and Matthew – we weren't a gang, not really, it was just a good name – *the gang of three.*

The lads are on the street.

PAST MARTIN   If her dad sees us, I'm dead, okay? So we   30
walk past –

MARK   And we make sure that she sees us –

MATTHEW   But we make sure that her dad *doesn't see us* making sure that *she sees us* –

MARK   And we hope that he doesn't *see her seeing*   35
us –

MATTHEW   We've done it a hundred times.

MARK   We know the score.

MATTHEW   Why don't you just come out with it and 'go public' with her.   40

PAST MARTIN   I'm not good enough for his all-singing, all-dancing, all-acting, all-modelling daughter. I'm a bad boy.

MARK   You? *(gently mocking)* A bad boy!?

MATTHEW   *(seemingly out of nowhere)* How much does   45
she get for it?

PAST MARTIN   *(confused)* For what?

MATTHEW   For the acting, the modelling and that –

NATALIE   *(approaching) She* doesn't think it's any of your business, Mark Thorpe. And at the   50
moment, *she* hardly gets any of it, because her mum puts it all in a sort of trust for when *she* is eighteen. All right?

13

MATTHEW	*(a little embarrassed)* Hiya Nat.
PAST MARTIN	Hello darling. Give us a kiss. 55
NATALIE	Don't you 'darling' me – I saw you gawping in my window, my dad *will* notice one day – swear to God. *(kisses him on the cheek)* So, what's up tonight, I don't want to just walk up and down you know – I have better 60 things to do with my life.
MATTHEW	We could go to the Unity…?
PAST MARTIN	Church youth club? Table tennis, pool, tiddlywinks! Anyone who wants to spend their Friday night in a youth club run by a 65 'right-on, down-with-the-kids priest' needs to get a life, or a girlfriend.
NATALIE	I wouldn't mind having a look at the Bassment later, I've heard it's good.
PAST MARTIN	And be the only skinny white kids in a Rap 70 Club? I'll pass, thanks.
NATALIE	It's R&B and Hip-Hop too you know, all sorts.
PAST MARTIN	Exactly – all black music!
NATALIE	If you hadn't noticed, nearly all music is black music. Except Beethoven and opera 75 and stuff.
MATTHEW	She's got a point there.
NATALIE	And it's you that's got a problem with colour. You shouldn't judge a person by what they look like. 80
PAST MARTIN	That, Natalie, is human nature, just human nature, pure and simple, and you can't change it. And anyway, who wants to do any of that when the fair is in town?

Sudden switch to the hospital bed, sound of monitors beeping. Two Nurses attend Martin's bedside.

Scene 3

NURSE 1	How is that dressing looking?
NURSE 2	It's fine. Nice and clean – no major problems.
NURSE 1	We'll wait until later on to get him properly cleaned up.
NURSE 2	He's been lucky.
NURSE 1	He won't feel lucky when he wakes up.
NURSE 2	They never do.

A sound from Present Martin

NURSE 2	Looks like he's back with us.
NURSE 1	I'll get them. *(leaves to get the parents)*
NURSE 2	*(looking down at him, knowing the words will go unheard)* Welcome back, Martin Turner. You are a very fortunate young man.
NURSE 1	Mrs Turner, Mr Turner – he's waking up.
MUM	Thank God!

They approach the bed.

NURSE 1	I'll get Dr Owens. *(exit)*
MUM	Martin … Martin?
PRESENT MARTIN	Mum … Dad?
DAD	Are you okay, son?
NARRATIVE MARTIN	Odd, isn't it – that's always when you know you're not okay – when someone asks if you are.

Sudden movement and noise at the fair as Natalie and the gang of three enter.

Scene 4

STREET VOICE 1	Scream if you wanna go faster!
STREET VOICE 2	Last few cars now, step on up!
STREET VOICE 3	Try your luck, hook a duck! Every one a winner.
STREET VOICE 4	Shoot out the star and win a prize. You have a go mate, I can see your girlfriend wants the teddy for her bedroom!
STREET VOICE 5	Stay in your cars – have your money ready.
STREET VOICE 6	Hold tight, now! Hold tight.
ALL STREET VOICES	Scream if you wanna go faster!
NARRATIVE MARTIN	Wanstead Flats, just a patch of grassland on the edge of Epping Forest, but I've always loved it. The idea of a forest on the edge of the city. A place for adventure. And when the fair is on – well, it's a place to gather with the ego turned on full.
STREET VOICE 1	Like a Caribbean curry, or an Irish stew, the ingredients simmer together in the East End.
STREET VOICE 2	Sometimes mingling, sometimes remaining distinct. Sometimes overpowering, sometimes subtle. A particular, peculiar blend.
STREET VOICE 6	Chinese, Vietnamese, Indian, Polish, Latvian, Greek, Somalian and Turkish.
STREET VOICE 3	Christian, Muslim, Jew, Sikh and a dozen other faiths, some you've never heard of.

ALL STREET VOICES	Everyone needs to belong.
STREET VOICE 5	This place has been changing for hundreds of years, longer. And it's changing still.
STREET VOICE 4	The only thing that stayed the same in East London, was that nothing stayed the same for long.
NARRATIVE MARTIN	On nights like this the police were always there. A couple of vans on the side streets, a couple on foot. Trouble was never far away – and to me, well the police seemed, well … like a sport really. Like a challenge.
PAST MARTIN	Look, over there. The young one – I'll get him going.
MARK	Go for it.
NATALIE	Don't, Martin.
MATTHEW	What's the point?
MARK	The point is the crack, Matthew – the buzz!
MATTHEW	*The point is* they'll be on our case all evening if you give them a reason to.
PAST MARTIN	Matthew – you worry too much.
MATTHEW	Martin – you don't worry enough.
PAST MARTIN	*(mocking)* Thanks, Dad.
MATTHEW	Very funny.
NATALIE	Okay, lads, this is not my idea of fun, but you go ahead. I'm hooking up with the girls, but I guess I'll see you later.

Kisses Martin and heads off.

PAST MARTIN	You two, watch from here. See the master at work.

30

35

40

45

50

17

Past Martin goes up to the Officer with sudden pretended panic.

PAST MARTIN   Officer – I need your help. There's a   55
problem.

OFFICER   What is it, son?

PAST MARTIN   There's a bad scene happening, something
really bad is going to go down.

OFFICER   Calm down son, calm down. What exactly is   60
it you think is going on?

PAST MARTIN   There's a guy back there, all tooled up!

OFFICER   Tooled up?

PAST MARTIN   I've just seen him.

OFFICER   Armed, you reckon?   65

PAST MARTIN   I *know*, Officer – and not just some little
shooter either, a great big rifle thing. I
thought you should know.

OFFICER   Okay, hold on. *(gets on his radio)* All units, be
aware of a possible incident. *(to Past Martin)*   70
Where did you see this guy? Can you
describe him?

PAST MARTIN   About six foot. Leather jacket. Short hair.

OFFICER   Where is he now?

PAST MARTIN   He's still by the stand he was at before. He's   75
taking pot-shots at some little bit of card with
a star on it … looks like a crack shot.

OFFICER   What?

PAST MARTIN   But who knows what he might do next…
Although the rifle is chained to the counter,   80
so I guess…

OFFICER	*(into radio)* All units stand down. False alarm, repeat, false alarm. *(to Past Martin)* Now you listen to me –
PAST MARTIN	*(mock innocence)* Just trying to help, Officer… 85 *(more naturally)* Oh come on… can't you take a joke?

The Officer looks Past Martin up and down, sees the others at a distance. He beckons them closer. An ominous quiet.

OFFICER	I'm going to tell you a little-known fact about our legal system.
PAST MARTIN	What's that? 90
OFFICER	There is a thing we call 'wasting police time' and it could get you a night in the cells. All of you.
MATTHEW	Sorry.
OFFICER	Good. Now you – *(to Martin)* what's your 95 name?
MARK	Don't tell him, Martin! *(realises his mistake)* Oh!
PAST MARTIN	Thanks … *Mark.*
OFFICER	Thanks, lads. Now, Martin … Mark, I have bigger fish than you to fry tonight, and you 100 are very lucky we didn't have twenty officers down here within two minutes – could have made things turn very ugly very quickly. Understand?

The gang of three mumble a sort of 'yes'.

OFFICER	Right. I know your face now, Martin. I've 105 seen your type before, a hundred times. So I

don't want to see your face come past me again unless it's on some funfair ride or you're stuffing it with candyfloss, okay?

PAST MARTIN   Okay.   110

The Officer leaves. Past Martin waits until he has gone.

PAST MARTIN   How cool was that? How cool was I? Who's the daddy?

MATTHEW   Very funny.

PAST MARTIN   And thanks for your help – 'Don't tell him, Martin' – *(sarcastically)* genius.   115

MARK   Hey, I never said I was clever.

MATTHEW   Can we just enjoy the fair now, please?

PAST MARTIN   Matthew, you may not have noticed, but that's exactly what we have been doing.

A beat.

MARK   Dodgems?   120

MATTHEW & PAST MARTIN   Dodgems!

They run off. Focus switches to the hospital room, where Present Martin is sitting up.

Scene 5

DR OWENS   Hello Martin, Mr and Mrs Turner. My name is Doctor Owens. Is it okay if I have a word with you? There are some things that I need to talk to you about.

PRESENT MARTIN   Yes, okay.   5

DR OWENS	There will be a lot to take in, you'll have a lot to think about – just give it time to all sink in, okay? And come back to me with any worries, anything. Okay?	
MUM	Okay. Just tell us what happens next.	10
DR OWENS	The drugs Martin is on may be making him feel a little strange right now and he has probably lost track of time. It was early Saturday morning when you had the accident, Martin, and it's early Sunday evening now.	15
	You were really thrown around when the car rolled and received a few cuts and lots of bruises to your body but no broken bones. Two cuts needed stitches, both are on the bottom of your leg where the impact on the car door caused it to cut into you. There are some light burns to your hands, which should soon heal without treatment. But unfortunately your face came out the worst.	20
		25
PRESENT MARTIN	What?	
DR OWENS	You have what we call deeper partial-thickness burns, sometimes called deep dermal burns.	
PRESENT MARTIN	What…? My face?	30
DR OWENS	You may need some skin grafting. This is where we take skin from one part of your body and move it to your face…	
PRESENT MARTIN	What?	
DR OWENS	…but we will only do grafts with your consent.	35

PRESENT MARTIN	My face?
DR OWENS	Have you got any questions? Martin? Have you got any questions?
PRESENT MARTIN	What about Mark? 40
DR OWENS	Mark is fine. Just some scratches, bruises. Nothing major. He's already home.
PRESENT MARTIN	Oh … good.

Scene 6

STREET VOICE 3	Weekend spent, the days of holiday trickle past.
STREET VOICE 5	One day leaches into another.
STREET VOICE 1	Rain stopped play, and long lie-ins were the order of the day. 5
STREET VOICE 2	The hours just ticked by, gloriously wasted.
STREET VOICE 4	No one knew that these were the final hours of Martin's old life.
ALL STREET VOICES	No one ever knows what's around the corner.
STREET VOICE 6	What the new day may bring. 10
STREET VOICE 3	And Friday brings sun, Friday brings guys out in baggy shorts and baseball caps, Friday brings out girls in strappy tops and sunglasses. It brings out the attitude in all of them. 15
STREET VOICE 6	Friday makes the High Street, East 6, feel like the beach. Friday brings Natalie her chance to dance.

Natalie and the gang of three enter.

NATALIE	So, whatever you say – *I'm going.* I'm seeing the girls there, and if you three don't want to come then that's no problem. But I am not spending the night walking between the rec, the kebab shop and the Chinese take-away.
MATTHEW	How much does it cost?
NATALIE	It's only a fiver before ten.
MATTHEW	A fiver?!
NATALIE	And I get in free before ten as well.
MARK	Because?
NATALIE	Because I'm a girl and a club is nothing without girls, because guys never dance unless we do it first.
MATTHEW	I'm not dancing.
MARK	No one asked you.
PAST MARTIN	I wouldn't know how.
NATALIE	You of all people should know how.
PAST MARTIN	Why's that? I never go to clubs.
NATALIE	*(becoming quite serious)* But you really come alive on the gym mat – you're awesome, like another person. It's like you forget yourself.
PAST MARTIN	*(thinking about it)* I do – and I forget that people are watching.
NATALIE	And that's what it's like when I dance. I'm, like… *(tries to think of the right word)* transported.
PAST MARTIN	Transformed…?
NATALIE	Exactly, and that's why I want to go.

A beat.

MATTHEW	I haven't got a clue what you two are talking about – all I know is I've only got a fiver, so I won't have any money for a drink.
MARK	Unless you get in as a girl! We should put you in a dress, save you a bit of money. A little mini-skirt, suit you just right.
NATALIE	I'll get you a drink – and if we don't like it, we don't have to stay, okay?

50

Past Martin takes up a comical gangsta stance.

PAST MARTIN	Gang of three,
	Y'coming with me?
	We going to get on down to the rap party.
MATTHEW	*(hurriedly thinking of words)* Not going to the … chippy, not going to the pub, We're going on down to the … Bassment Club.
MARK	*(much more fluid)* We might enjoy it,
	We might just fit,
	It might be great, but it might be…*(the others wait for him to finish)* not half as good as we're hoping!

55

60

65

They all exit, laughing. Narrative Martin is standing looking over Past Martin in bed.

Scene 7

NARRATIVE MARTIN	I remember feeling the tightness in my face, feeling that I couldn't move parts of it. At first I thought I'll just feel it, with my hands. See if I can make sense of it with my fingers. *(Past Martin's hands go towards his face)* But

5

then I thought, I've seen the rest, the cuts,
bruises, the scratches – but I hadn't seen my
face. And I needed to. Whatever anyone said
– I needed to.

Present Martin begins to look around his room
from his bed, distractedly. Nurse 1 enters.

NURSE 1   How are we doing, Martin? Let me know if   10
you're uncomfortable and we'll see what we
can do for you, okay? Not long until dinner
now – have you written down what you
wanted – ? Martin. Martin – what's up?

PRESENT MARTIN   There's no mirror in this room, is there?   15

NURSE 1   *(after a short, awkward pause)* No, Martin. You
see, with cases like yours –

PRESENT MARTIN   I want a mirror.

NURSE 1   Sometimes it's better if –

PRESENT MARTIN   I want a mirror.   20

NURSE 1   Martin –

PRESENT MARTIN   I want to see my face.

A beat.

NURSE 1   Okay.

PRESENT MARTIN   Thank you.

Scene 8

Sudden loud dance music, over which Martin has
to struggle to be heard.

PAST MARTIN   I thought it was in a basement?!

MARK   So did I.

NATALIE	What?
PAST MARTIN	It's called the Basement – I thought it was in a basement. 5
NATALIE	Bass. Martin, 'bass' B – A – S – S.
MATTHEW	As in Drum and Bass, as in treble and bass – twit!
PAST MARTIN	I get it – I'm not stupid!
NATALIE	And look, Martin, not all the people are 10 black, look, there's a white boy, gosh can you believe it, and a white girl. And another – and…
PAST MARTIN	Okay, don't rub it in. You want a drink?
NATALIE	What a gentleman – just a Coke, thanks. 15

Martin goes off with Mark and Matthew.

MARCIA	Hiya. What's happening?
NATALIE	Just watching. Just listening.
MARCIA	Safe.
NATALIE	Do I know you – I kind of know the face…?
MARCIA	I dunno, have you been here before? 20
NATALIE	No, it's my first time here.
MARCIA	You like it?
NATALIE	Well, we've only just come, but it looks alright. Yeah. I like it.
MARCIA	I love it here, I come here all the time. 25 Who you with?
NATALIE	Those three.
MARCIA	Oh yeah, so which one's ya boyfriend then? One of them is always the boyfriend.

NATALIE	In the middle.	30
MARCIA	Nice face. Good-looking guy. What's his name?	
NATALIE	Martin. *(suddenly realises)* Hey, hands off, lady!	
MARCIA	It's cool – he's *your* man. I ain't no thief!	35
NATALIE	So … who are *you* here with?	
MARCIA	Ah, I come here on me own, but I know loads of people here, I got no problems here, we're all cool, like a big family, you know what I'm saying?	40
NATALIE	Yeah – that's good.	
MARCIA	*(struggling to hear)* What?	
NATALIE	*(calling out)* I said 'that's good'.	
MARCIA	Look, I'm gonna circulate. I'll see you later.	
NATALIE	Okay, nice talking to you, see you. Hey, what's your name?	45
MARCIA	Marcia.	
NATALIE	My name's Natalie, see you later.	

The guys return, Past Martin has a lager in his hand.

PAST MARTIN	Who was that you were talking to?	
NATALIE	She's really nice, her name's Marcia.	50
PAST MARTIN	What?	
NATALIE	Marcia!	
PAST MARTIN	I didn't know you had friends here.	
NATALIE	I have now, haven't I? And what are you doing? You don't drink.	55

PAST MARTIN	This isn't drinking. I'm not going to get drunk on this stuff.
NATALIE	You can. Lightweight. I've seen you drunk on lemonade!
PAST MARTIN	Don't be silly. Have a sip. 60
NATALIE	I'll stick with my Coke, thanks.

The four stand watching the dance floor.

STREET VOICE 1	Clock ticks, drowned out by infectious beat plus alcohol in the bloodstream – eventually makes things look more – relaxed.
PAST MARTIN	Hey Nat … fancy a dance? 65
NATALIE	What, with you? You don't dance.
STREET VOICE 2	Coloured light throwing stark shadow on jet black wall eventually makes things look more – exciting.
PAST MARTIN	But *you* do – I will if you do. 70
NATALIE	I don't fancy it yet – maybe later.
STREET VOICE 3	Sweat and breath of a hundred bodies eventually makes the place seem – safe.
PAST MARTIN	What about you?
MARK	Are you mad!? I dance like I've got some mad person pulling my strings. 75
MATTHEW	And don't even look at me.
STREET VOICE 4	And the bass, the bass, the bass, in his chest and his brain finally makes the floor look more – inviting. 80
PAST MARTIN	Okay – cowards. Here, hold my drink.
STREET VOICE 5	And the space, the space that opened up,

just there and just then, finally, seemed like the very place to be, at the very time.

STREET VOICE 6   Come the moment – come the man.   85

PAST MARTIN   I'm going in!

Sudden silence and stillness.

Scene 9

NARRATIVE MARTIN   I could see it. The moment the doctor came in I knew it was there. Under a towel all right, but I knew what it was. It was under there.

DR OWENS   Now Martin, I am sure you know that you   5
have every right to a mirror but it has to be said that, in my opinion, it's a little early for that. I would suggest that you give it at least a couple of days. Sometimes it helps to prepare yourself, to get used to the idea.   10

PRESENT MARTIN   Of?

DR OWENS   The idea of, your … condition.

PRESENT MARTIN   I want the mirror now.

DR OWENS   I've spoken to your parents and they are, frankly, concerned that you want a mirror   15
so early. But they also said that once you make up your mind to do something, then there's no stopping you.

PRESENT MARTIN   Good. And I have made up my mind.

DR OWENS   Martin, have you ever seen someone with   20
facial burns?

PRESENT MARTIN   No.

DR OWENS	Have you ever seen anyone who has been badly burned at all?
PRESENT MARTIN	No, only in films. 25
DR OWENS	This isn't a film, Martin.
PRESENT MARTIN	I'm not stupid.
DR OWENS	I know. But I need to warn you that when you look in the mirror you may be quite … shocked at what you see. Whatever you see 30 will be improved on in time. But Martin, you must know that you will always have some scarring on your face. Your face will never be as it was. *Even if* a graft is successful.
PRESENT MARTIN	I understand. 35
DR OWENS	Is there anything at all I can do for you now? Is there anything you need?
PRESENT MARTIN	Just the mirror.
DR OWENS	Okay. So, here we go. Now Martin, take hold of it, that's right, just keep it held down for a 40 second and take a deep breath. Sometimes it's best to have a quick glance, look away, and then have a longer look.

Martin begins to get out of the bed.

DR OWENS	What are you doing?
PRESENT MARTIN	I want to see it in the light – open the 45 curtain, please.

He walks to the window and Narrative Martin becomes his reflection. Slowly he looks at himself.

NARRATIVE MARTIN	The whites of my eyes were –
PRESENT MARTIN	Red.

NARRATIVE MARTIN	My skin looked so rough –	
PRESENT MARTIN	So uneven.	50
NARRATIVE MARTIN	Bright red in places, and then there was –	
PRESENT MARTIN	Brown, pinky-white.	
NARRATIVE MARTIN	The underneath was on top.	
PRESENT MARTIN	Veins showing through.	
NARRATIVE MARTIN	So swollen.	55
PRESENT MARTIN	So blistered.	
NARRATIVE MARTIN	And my hair, at the top, at the front –	
PRESENT MARTIN	Mostly gone –	
NARRATIVE MARTIN	Just patches.	
PRESENT MARTIN	Like a doll…	60
NARRATIVE MARTIN	…that had been in a fire. I remember thinking –	
PRESENT MARTIN	Is that me?	
NARRATIVE MARTIN	And I thought.	
PRESENT MARTIN	Will it fall off?	65
NARRATIVE MARTIN	It seems stupid now.	
PRESENT MARTIN	Will my real face be underneath?	
NARRATIVE MARTIN	And then, weird, I remembered being in a plane on my way to Spain, looking down on mountains from far, far above. That's what my face looked like –	70
PRESENT MARTIN	A mountain.	
NARRATIVE MARTIN	Rough, and ruptured and jagged and sharp and solid. Not like skin, not like a face, not like me.	75
PRESENT MARTIN	Not like me.	

31

DR OWENS	I'm sorry, Martin.

Present Martin puts the mirror down and Narrative Martin steps away. Present Martin curls up on his bed.

Scene 10

Narrative Martin looks over at himself at the club. Past Martin and others at the club take up the first of a number of still images which illustrate the development of the dance, almost like snapshots.

NARRATIVE MARTIN	Look at me. I had no idea. *(calls to his past self)* It's all over, Martin. All over! Listen to me! You fool. You stupid fool! *(he softens, looks to the audience)* Oh bless … all I wanted to do was dance.	5
STREET VOICES 1, 2 & 3	It's a formula you can't fault.	
STREET VOICES 4, 5 & 6	'Gymnast' plus 'rhythm' equals 'dancer'.	
NARRATIVE MARTIN	That night, for the first time, I suddenly knew I could do it. If I could free myself from worrying about people watching, I could do it.	10
ALL STREET VOICES	Just forget that people are watching.	
NARRATIVE MARTIN	And I did. Nervous at first, but then – one two, left right, one two, right left. Things were going okay and then – *I put my hands in the air.*	15

New image.

No, no hands in the air, I look like a raver
and I don't want to look like a raver in this
bad ass rap club. One two, left right, one
two, right left. No, going wrong,   20
thinking too much, look like Cliff Richard,
I'm dancing like an uncle at a wedding. And
everyone's looking at me, and woh! … there
go my hands again, what can I do with my
hands?   25

New image.

Not going well, Nat and Mark and Matthew,
looking embarrassed. Oh no! New guy in the
ring.

New image, Past Martin is joined by another
dancer.

He came out of nowhere – and he was good,
smooth, supple, confident, cocky and he   30
took over, just plain took over.

New image.

And then – and then – I thought, 'I can do
that'. I'm a gymnast – I can do that and
better. I've done moves like that, harder than
that, for years. Okay, here we go, one, two,   35
three and bounce and splits and yeah man,
one, two, three and splits and bounce and
yeah I got it going on, one, two, three.
Crowd clapping. Nat looking proud, yeah
dead proud, and me just moving like on the   40
gym mat. In the zone. All eyes on me and
me in some other place somehow – distant.
Transported. Transformed.

New image.

The white boy *can dance*. Hands down, to
the left, to the right, head roll, and down   45
for the splits, and moonwalk, moonwalk,
moonwalk. Forward, forward, and now, can I
do this, yeah I can do it, full somersault time,
here we go, one, two, three and…

Big intake of breath from all watching.

…perfect landing, and muscle-man pose.   50

*Massive roars from crowd with clapping. Music
comes in loud again.*

PAST MARTIN *(calling over the music)* Who's the daddy!?
Who's the daddy!?

Scene 11

*Sudden freeze, mood change. Natalie, Mark and
Matthew line up with Mum and Dad and Dr Owens.
Slowly we see Present Martin sit up on the side of
his bed for the first time.*

NARRATIVE MARTIN It's strange, and I didn't know this before,
but 'hospital time' is different. Hospital time
stretches days, makes them drag and crawl. I
forget what happened on which day now…
There were visits…   5

NATALIE Does it hurt?

MARK We thought you weren't going to – well you
know.

NATALIE What's the food like in here then?

MARK	It was all in the paper you know. You're famous!	10
NATALIE	Do you get your own telly – what channels can you have?	
MARK	I'll bring some music in for you shall I – I've got some new stuff, you'll love it.	15
PRESENT MARTIN	*(to Matthew)* You're very quiet.	
MATTHEW	I'm sorry but – what can I say, look at you. And I know you don't want to hear this, none of you do, *but I told you. I told you.*	
PRESENT MARTIN	Is that all you can say?	20
MATTHEW	You should hear it – from a friend.	
	A beat.	
PRESENT MARTIN	Do I get a kiss, then?	
	Awkward pause. Natalie, Mark and Matthew exit.	
NARRATIVE MARTIN	And Mum and Dad were there loads. I'd wake up and there they'd be – bless them. With chit chat and DVDs and sweets and magazines and news.	25
DAD	You're just as well off in here son, the weather's awful.	
MUM	Auntie Sue sent a card this morning – she won't be able to get to see you because of her hip, but she sent some stuff for you too.	30
DAD	The car was a pig to start this morning – you know how it is sometimes.	
MUM	Your form tutor sent a letter asking us to go and talk to them about you not falling behind – can't afford to do that.	35

35

DAD	Dave from work says hello – says he'll pop by with some game or other. Says you said you liked it.
MUM	Oh … and … we heard this morning. 40 Thought you should know. That bloke…
DAD	Pete.
MUM	He didn't make it. I know I should feel sorry for him – but what he did to you –
DAD	He didn't do it! 45
MUM	I only feel for his poor family.
DAD	No one deserves that.

They exit.

NARRATIVE MARTIN	And the op – the graft.
DR OWENS	Good morning. *(looks at a chart)* Patient B503.
PRESENT MARTIN	I am not a number – I am a free man! 50
DR OWENS	We need to make sure you are who we think you are – this is a big place and if there were two Martin Turners in it you might end up with no appendix while he gets a skin graft! Fancy that? 55
PRESENT MARTIN	Okay! I'll be Patient B503 then, just for today.
DR OWENS	Now, you haven't eaten since last night?
PRESENT MARTIN	Nope.
DR OWENS	And you know the procedure? We'll give you an anaesthetic up here, take you to theatre, 60 and you'll be with us for a couple of hours – we take healthy tissue from your thigh and apply it on the burn area. Then you'll wake up, back in your bed, this evening.

PRESENT MARTIN	And then I look like Brad Pitt?	65
DR OWENS	It's a surgical procedure – not a miracle! In all seriousness, Martin, things will never be the same again.	
PRESENT MARTIN	I know.	
DR OWENS	The anaesthetic is pretty painless – but you may feel a little prick –	70
PRESENT MARTIN	Doctor!	
DR OWENS	Believe me, Martin – *I have* heard that one before!	
NARRATIVE MARTIN	And it didn't work miracles, and I didn't look like Brad Pitt. And it did hurt. But the next day, the day after the op – I thought I'd better take a first step back towards the real world. Well, out of my room at least. Time to face the world.	75 80

Scene 12

Present Martin gets up from his bed for the first time. The Street Voices, all wearing masks indicating burns or disfigurement, take up places on the stage. They read, listen to music, do crosswords, but pay him little attention as he walks by.

NARRATIVE MARTIN	I didn't get it at first – didn't get why they weren't staring, why they weren't shocked.	

Anthony approaches.

ANTHONY	Alright, guy, how you going? Nice to see you.	
PRESENT MARTIN	*(gasps when he sees Anthony's face)* Oh wow – erm – hello. Look, I'm sorry, I'm really sorry.	5

ANTHONY	*(with a breezy, easy manner)* It's alright, I'm used to it. We all get used to it. You're Martin aren't you?
PRESENT MARTIN	Yes – how do you know my name?
ANTHONY	One of the nurses told me about you, said you were a West Ham fan.
PRESENT MARTIN	Are you?
ANTHONY	No – *I like football!*
PRESENT MARTIN	Very funny.
ANTHONY	Spurs me. Tottenham all the way!
PRESENT MARTIN	*(goading him)* Oh right – I have heard the name, I wasn't sure they were still going! Spurs are a charity case.
ANTHONY	Look who's talking. Come on then – what happened to you?
PRESENT MARTIN	Oh. *(surprised at the directness of the question)* I was in a car crash – the car caught fire.
ANTHONY	Right. How long have you been here?
PRESENT MARTIN	Just over a week – I had a graft yesterday. How long have you been here?
ANTHONY	Well it's a long story – I was born like this – well not like this – but I was born with what they call severe facial disfigurements blah, blah, blah. I've been in here six times and I've had eight operations. I could stay on any ward if I wanted to but I like staying on this one. All the nurses here know me and I like them.
PRESENT MARTIN	Yeah, they're nice.
ANTHONY	And this is the one place in the world where no one cares what you look like!

STREET VOICES	*(off)* Everyone needs to belong.	
ANTHONY	I've just had an operation a couple of days ago and I'm going home today.	
PRESENT MARTIN	Did you say 'eight operations'!?	40
ANTHONY	That's right, some were for plastic surgery, but most of them were to help me breathe and see better.	
PRESENT MARTIN	What's your name?	
ANTHONY	Anthony. Where's your bed?	45
PRESENT MARTIN	I got my own room, down there.	
ANTHONY	Oh yeah, that's right. I was in that room once, it's alright in there.	
PRESENT MARTIN	Do you want to see it again?	
ANTHONY	Yeah, I haven't been in it for ages.	50
PRESENT MARTIN	Okay. *(they begin to walk together)*	
ANTHONY	Hello Karl.	
STREET VOICE 1	Alright, Anthony, how you going?	
ANTHONY	Not too bad thanks. Hey Tommy, what's up, man?	55
STREET VOICE 2	Hiya guy, what you up to?	
ANTHONY	You know me, just cruising. Checking out the joint.	
STREET VOICE 3	We know you all right, you just stay away from the ladies.	60
STREET VOICE 4	Don't listen to him Anthony, don't you stay away from the ladies.	
ANTHONY	I won't, I'll be coming to see you later, Carol. Stay cool.	

STREET VOICE 4	Can't wait.	65
STREET VOICE 5	Enough already – you're making me want to be sick!	
STREET VOICE 6	Have you seen what's on the menu for today – that'll make you sick, mate!	

Laughter from the ward as Anthony and Present Martin enter his room.

ANTHONY	Yeah, my old room. See you got a few West Ham books there. Your iPod is it? What you listening to?	70
PRESENT MARTIN	A bit of this – a bit of that.	
ANTHONY	I think music keeps you sane. Is that your parents in that photo?	75
PRESENT MARTIN	Yeah, like I'm going to forget what they look like, just because I'm in here.	
ANTHONY	Parents are funny like that. Don't forget, this didn't just happen to you, they're in it too.	
PRESENT MARTIN	I guess.	80
ANTHONY	And is that your sister?	
PRESENT MARTIN	No man, that's my girl.	
ANTHONY	What, your *girlfriend*?	
PRESENT MARTIN	Yeah, man.	
ANTHONY	What's her name?	85
PRESENT MARTIN	Natalie.	
ANTHONY	She's not bad, nice face. *(a beat)* So … is she sticking by you?	
PRESENT MARTIN	What do you mean?	
ANTHONY	Is she still going to hang out with you when you get out? Some girls don't, you know.	90

Some girls back off, they start saying things like 'let's just be friends' or 'we're getting too serious' and things like that, but we all know what they mean.   95

PRESENT MARTIN She's sticking by me alright, she was here yesterday.

ANTHONY Shame.

PRESENT MARTIN What's a shame?

ANTHONY It's a shame I didn't see her, you know what 100 I mean, brighten up her day, bring a smile to her face, you get me?

PRESENT MARTIN Yeah, I get you.

ANTHONY Hey, I've got to go, my mum will be here soon. I'm glad your operation went well.   105 You'll be okay, they're good here, the best. And listen, a word from the wise: whatever happens on here *(pointing to his face)* nothing has changed in here *(points to his brain)* or in here *(points to his heart)*. People will stare – 110 they will do that for the rest of your life. The problem is with *them*, not with *you*. You have to hang in there. They'll tire of it soon enough. You've just got to know, everything is different now – you're not in Kansas any 115 more.

PRESENT MARTIN Kansas?

ANTHONY Ask your mum. Look, I'll see you around. Say 'hello' to Natalie for me.

Anthony exits, Narrative Martin watches him go.

PRESENT MARTIN *(laughing to himself)* Kansas!?   120

NARRATIVE MARTIN & PRESENT MARTIN	What a guy.
NARRATIVE MARTIN	Who would have thought it? In this place of all places, with all this to deal with – who'd have thought that I'd find a friend.

Scene 13

Present Martin sits on his bed, Mum and Dad sit by it, the Officer approaches.

OFFICER	Mr Turner, Mrs Turner. My name is Constable Lincoln. I know that Martin has been through a lot, but it's time to get a bit of information from him.	
MUM	The poor lad is barely back on his feet – he's just had an operation.	5
OFFICER	I realise that it will be painful to live through it all again –	
MUM	Then give him a break!	
OFFICER	– but we have to know the facts. We need to know what he knows.	10
DAD	Listen, love, the Officer is just doing a job. *(to the Officer)* I take it we can stay?	
OFFICER	By all means. I'll be as quick as I can. Trust me.	15
MUM	Just make it quick, okay?	
OFFICER	Okay. *(approaching Present Martin, checking notes)* Martin, I'm Constable Lincoln. I have a few questions to ask you about Friday night and Saturday morning. Just be as honest and as clear as you can be – I know some	20

	things may be a bit fuzzy, but just do your best. And if you remember anything after I've gone, then just give me a call, okay?	
PRESENT MARTIN	You don't remember me, do you?	25
OFFICER	*(baffled)* Should I?	
MUM	What's going on, Martin?	
PRESENT MARTIN	The last time you saw me you said – let me make sure I remember it right – you said:	
PAST & NARRATIVE MARTIN	'I don't want to see your face come past me again unless it's on some funfair ride or you're stuffing it with candyfloss, okay?'	30
OFFICER	That was you?	
PRESENT MARTIN	That was me.	
OFFICER	I didn't –	35
PRESENT MARTIN	No. I look different.	
OFFICER	Yes, you do.	
MUM	*(trying to break an awkward moment)* Are you okay to carry on, Martin?	
PRESENT MARTIN	I'm okay. Let's do this and get it over with.	40
OFFICER	Just take me through it – in your own time.	
PRESENT MARTIN	It seems so long ago now. But I do remember. We were all at the Bassment. Just dancing, chatting. A good night. And at the end of it we all made our way out…	45
NATALIE	I knew you'd like it. I had a great time and I'm going to go back.	
PAST MARTIN	See you tomorrow, then. Give us a kiss.	
NATALIE	Martin, give it a rest.	
MATTHEW	Don't worry about me, I'll wait down there.	50

PAST MARTIN	Give us a kiss. *(they kiss)* Nice one. More.
NATALIE	I'll give you more tomorrow if you teach me some of them dance moves.
PAST MARTIN	You got yourself a deal there.
NATALIE	See you tomorrow. 55
PRESENT MARTIN	…and Nat went off with some friends, and me and Matthew and Mark went down the high street.
STREET VOICE 1	Chip shop, kebab van, working girl, pusher. A different side, just coming to life. Another 60 East Ham, just waking up.
PUSHER	Hey, boys, surely you're not going home yet? I got goodies if you need some inspiration, some energy. Make you the life and soul. I got E's at prices no one can beat and if 65 you're into a bit of coke or smack give me fifteen minutes and I can do ya a bargain. You won't get a better deal here.
PAST MARTIN	No thanks.
PUSHER	It's top-quality stuff, guy! Check it out, great 70 gear, great prices. Make you smile clear into next week!
PAST MARTIN	Clear off, mate.
PUSHER	What?! Who ya talking to?
PAST MARTIN	I'm talking to you, scum. Get out of my way. 75
PUSHER	That's dead-man talk. Be careful, you don't know me, I take no prisoners, so respect your elders, baby boy. Schoolboy.

MATTHEW	*(in Martin's ear)* Leave it, Martin. Let's go. This is not worth it.

80

PUSHER	I hope you're giving him good advice.
MATTHEW	I am. Come on Martin, let's walk.
PUSHER	That's right, walk. Whatever happens, don't mess with me, schoolboy, cause I don't mess. I cut flesh like you every day.

85

The three walk off, Past Martin shouts back:

PAST MARTIN	Get lost!
PRESENT MARTIN	So yes, I had had a few lagers, but no, I hadn't taken anything – before you ask. Just say 'no' eh?
OFFICER	And then?

90

PRESENT MARTIN	Then we cut through the estate. To get to Green Street. That's when we saw them, well, we heard them first.

As the Street Voices speak they set out four chairs as the car.

STREET VOICE 2	The screech of tyre on tarmac. The roar of engine at full throttle.

95

STREET VOICE 3	The thump, thump, thump of music from window. Drive by once –
MARK	*(as if just missed by the car)* Oi!
MATTHEW	*(shouting at the car as it goes by)* Watch it!
STREET VOICE 4	– pass and on down the road. And then – handbrake turn.

100

STREET VOICE 5	Calm, quiet, engine idling, music, muffled.
PAST MARTIN	This doesn't look good.

MATTHEW	Oh, no!
STREET VOICE 6	And spring back to life and back, back. 105 Faster, faster. And brake and skid and – stop.

Apache and Pete take up the front seats.

PETE	Evening, lads.
PAST MARTIN	Pete! What the…?
OFFICER	You do realise, Martin, that Peter Mosley … never regained consciousness? 110
MUM	Martin knows that he … didn't make it.
PRESENT MARTIN	The word is 'died' mum. He died.
PAST MARTIN	You scared me.
PETE	Just a bit of fun!
MATTHEW	Doesn't seem like fun from the pavement. 115
PETE	Me and Apache are just out for a drive. Fancy a spin?
MARK	'Apache' – what kind of name is that?
PETE	*(whispering)* We don't take the mick out of Apache's name, okay? 120
MATTHEW	Okay, but I don't *drive* with Apache either.
PETE	Whatever – you guys?
PAST MARTIN	We're just on our way home, Pete. Thanks.
PETE	Then we'll drop you.
MARK	Really? 125
MATTHEW	Mark!
PAST MARTIN	Would you?
MATTHEW	Martin!
PAST MARTIN	Like I said before, Matthew, you worry too much. 130

MATTHEW	And you –
PAST MARTIN	*(stopping him short)* Yeah, you told me already.

An awkward pause.

APACHE	*(sharply)* Well get in if you're getting in, this bus is pulling out!	
PAST MARTIN	Alright, just a lift home.	135
MATTHEW	*(furious)* Are you really going? You're mad, you're off your head Martin, *don't go*.	
PAST MARTIN	It's just a lift home, we'll be there in five minutes, less. It's much quicker than walking.	140
MATTHEW	Why are you even opening the door?	
PAST MARTIN	Come on, man. I'm sick of walking.	
MATTHEW	I don't believe this. Do you trust him? Martin, come on, let's walk.	
PAST MARTIN	It's cool, we'll be fine.	145
MATTHEW	Okay Martin, you go. I'm off – but I'm telling ya, I think you're mad. Later.	
PAST MARTIN	Come on Matthew.	
MATTHEW	I said later.	

Past Martin and Mark climb in – Matthew exits.

OFFICER	So Matthew Thorpe never even got in the car?	150
PRESENT MARTIN	Never even got in. Just me and Mark.	
ALL STREET VOICES	No one ever knows what's around the next corner.	
OFFICER	And then?	
PRESENT MARTIN	Then it started…	155

PETE	Let's see what this thing can do!
APACHE	The night is young!
PETE	And so are we!
PRESENT MARTIN	They never meant to just take us home...
PAST MARTIN	Apache, man, you're going the wrong way. 160
APACHE	It's cool, guy, I got it covered.
MARK	I don't like this.
PAST MARTIN	I don't care how covered you got it, you're going the wrong way.
PETE	Relax. 165
PAST MARTIN	Never mind relax, let's turn back.
APACHE	You never mind, these are the good times, chill out.
PAST MARTIN	Please, man, let's go back. I gotta get home.
MARK	Please, mate. We just want to get back. 170
APACHE	Get real, it's me, Apache, remember my motto: 'No surrender – no mercy!'
MARK	No brains!
PETE	Watch it, you!
PAST MARTIN	What are you talking about 'no mercy'. I just 175 wanted a lift.
APACHE	And you're getting one –
PAST MARTIN	*(to Pete)* Is he on something?
PETE	Hey! Don't grind the gears, man!
APACHE	Well excuse me – I have to get used to this 180 car – I've only had it ten minutes!
MARK	Did he say 'ten minutes'?
PAST MARTIN	What do you mean 'ten minutes'?! You nicked it, didn't you?

APACHE	Do you think I'd buy a heap like this? The engine in this thing is like a washing machine. I only nicked it cause I can't stand the owner.	185
PAST MARTIN	Take me home, man, in fact forget home, just leave me here.	190
MARK	Yeah, just here is fine!	
APACHE	Enjoy the ride and stop being so stressed out, will ya.	
PAST MARTIN	I'm not stressed. I just wanna go home.	
PRESENT MARTIN	Then there was the flashing light, just like something from off the TV. They were right behind us…	195
PETE	Oh no. Coppers, there's cops behind us.	
PAST MARTIN	They're flashing their headlights.	
MARK	You'll have to stop.	200
APACHE	They can do what they want to do, we're going.	
PAST MARTIN	Stop the car.	
PETE	Shut up!	
PRESENT MARTIN	And then Pete threw something out of the window, a sort of package, a small bag or something. I didn't see clearly…	205
MARK	What was that you just threw out?	
PETE	I'll show you in five minutes – when we get rid of these pigs, we'll come back for it.	
PAST MARTIN	Let us get out. You can do what you want to but let us out.	210
APACHE	This is a laugh, guy. They can't get us, their cars may be better but they're crap drivers.	

PAST MARTIN	This is not fair, Pete – you didn't say it was nicked, you didn't say you had anything on you!
	215
PETE	I haven't now, have I? And who said anything about 'fair'? We're not stopping now.
ALL STREET VOICES	No one ever knows what's around the next corner.
	220
PAST MARTIN	Traffic lights.
PRESENT MARTIN	On red.
MARK	Look, traffic lights.
PRESENT MARTIN	Big van coming through.
PAST MARTIN	STOP! STOP!
	225
APACHE	I'm going for it, guy. No surrender! No mercy!!

Silence. All those in the car calmly place themselves in positions as if after the crash. Present Martin gets up from his bed and surveys the scene.

PRESENT MARTIN	I remember heat and pain. People shouting. Lights. But the heat, the heat I remember most. And then nothing.
	230

All Street Voices walk in and carry Past Martin to the hospital bed, gently lay him down and place a mask on his face. Present Martin watches.

PRESENT MARTIN	The next thing I knew. I was here.
MUM	That's enough now –
OFFICER	We may need to speak to him again.
DAD	He's going home today.

MUM   You know where we live.   235

DAD   He's not going anywhere.

OFFICER Thank you. We'll speak soon. *(exits)*

MUM   Are you ready to go, son?

Narrative and Present Martin stare at Past Martin on the bed.

DAD   Are you okay, son?   240

Act Two

Scene 1

Present Martin in his room, again looking at his reflection.

NARRATIVE MARTIN I've looked in mirrors for years. I've always liked looking in them – always liked what I saw. Before, the thing that looked back always looked like me. So how, when the thing looking back looked nothing like me – 5 could I still be me? Was I the same me, or a different me? A worse me or a better me?

STREET VOICE 1 Home, back in the bosom of his family, in the place he knows best.

STREET VOICE 2 No more white tiles and beds on wheels and 10 curtains.

STREET VOICE 3 No more strange smells and odd noises in the night. No bleeps and drips and coughs and whispered encouragement.

STREET VOICE 4 Just the security of his things, in his place, 15 just as they were.

STREET VOICE 5 Everything as it should be, just as it was on that night he went out.

STREET VOICE 6 Everything just the same, everything so different. 20

STREET VOICE 1 Mum and Dad out at work – nice day outside. But not nice enough to want to go out. Not ready to be seen. Not yet. Not by the public.

STREET VOICE 6 So the face stays inside. Hiding from the world, facing only itself. 25

ALL STREET VOICES	And it's quiet.

A lull, then the sound of a doorbell.

STREET VOICE 1	Panic! Could be anyone.	
STREET VOICE 2	Not expecting anyone.	
STREET VOICE 3	Could ignore it.	
STREET VOICE 4	The coward's way out.	30
STREET VOICE 5	Could be Nat, or Mark or Matt.	
STREET VOICE 6	Have to answer it.	
ALL STREET VOICES	Face the world.	

Present Martin opens the door a little.

FORM TUTOR	Martin, is that you? I'm glad I found you in.	
PRESENT MARTIN	My mum and dad aren't here.	35
FORM TUTOR	That's okay – I know it seems odd, your form teacher on your doorstep, but I thought perhaps we should talk about what you want to do about returning.	
PRESENT MARTIN	Returning?	40
FORM TUTOR	How long you want to leave it. We understand that you may not feel ready to 'hit the ground running' at the start of term, so perhaps you'd like work sent home until you feel more – prepared, when things have calmed down a little, when the other students have had a chance to get used to – the new situation.	45
NARRATIVE MARTIN	It was *almost* sweet – and I was so tempted to say I needed the rest of term off, to hide in my room and get on with things in secret,	50

to turn my face away. But then I thought,
'What would Anthony do?'

ANTHONY *(walking through, unobserved)* People will stare
– they will do that for the rest of your life.   55

NARRATIVE MARTIN How would he deal with this?

ANTHONY The problem is with them, not with you.

NARRATIVE MARTIN What would he tell them all?

ANTHONY You have to hang in there. *(exits)*

NARRATIVE MARTIN And it was suddenly very clear.   60

PRESENT MARTIN *(opens door wide)* Term starts on Monday, yes?

FORM TUTOR *(surprised)* Yes, that's right.

PRESENT MARTIN Then I'd best be there, I guess.

FORM TUTOR Martin, do you think that's – ?

PRESENT MARTIN *(sharply, indignantly)* Yes, I do. I'm not going   65
to hide. And I'm not going to wait until
you've had a chance to do a nice assembly
on me and what's happened. I'm not
ashamed. I didn't do anything wrong, I just
made a mistake, and I'm paying for it enough   70
as it is, thank you very much. My brain still
works – it's just the face that's changed and
the sooner people get used to that, the better.

FORM TUTOR Perhaps your parents might like to –

PRESENT MARTIN You ask them if you want, but they know   75
that when I've made up my mind, that's it.

FORM TUTOR It may be hard for you at first.

PRESENT MARTIN *Whenever* I come back it will be hard. Next
Monday or the Monday after that, or the one
after that. There has to be a first day – I'd   80
rather get it over and done with.

FORM TUTOR	If you're sure.
PRESENT MARTIN	I'm sure *(softening a little)* but thanks for asking, anyway. See you then.
FORM TUTOR	Good luck, Martin. 85

Martin goes inside and gets out his phone, dials. Natalie enters and answers.

NATALIE	Hiya.
PRESENT MARTIN	Guess what?
NATALIE	What?
PRESENT MARTIN	I'm going to school on Monday.
NATALIE	*(haltingly)* You? School? Monday?! 90
PRESENT MARTIN	*(gently mocking her)* Yes! That's! Right!
NATALIE	*(surprised)* Who said you could?
PRESENT MARTIN	I said. No one has said I can't. So tell Matthew. Come and call for me on your way. We can go together if that's cool. 95
NATALIE	Are you sure you want to go back so soon?
PRESENT MARTIN	What do you mean 'so soon'? Everyone else is going back, so I'm going back.
NATALIE	But you're not everyone else. You can't just rush into things, you know. 100
PRESENT MARTIN	What? I thought you'd be pleased.
NATALIE	Shouldn't you be resting, recuperating or whatever they call it? It seems very soon to me.
PRESENT MARTIN	Nat, you do realise that you're supposed to 105 be supporting me? You should be helping me. Not telling me to hide away. You're my

girl. I'll need you and Mark and Matthew to help me. It's not going to be easy. But what are friends for? I thought friends were 110 supposed to stick together and help each other out. If I want to go back to school you should be happy for me, you should be saying, 'Yeah Martin, go for it'.

NATALIE   Okay, okay, I just think you should be 115 taking it easy.

PRESENT MARTIN   Will you knock for me on Monday morning or not?

NATALIE   Yes, I'll be there. I'll be speaking to Matthew later. See you on Monday. 120

PRESENT MARTIN   Nat!?

NATALIE   What?

PRESENT MARTIN   Aren't you even going to ask me how I am?

NATALIE   Yeah, of course. How are you?

PRESENT MARTIN   I'm back. 125

Scene 2

STREET VOICE 1   Back to normal. Bright sunny Monday morning.

NARRATIVE MARTIN   The smell of toast. Mum calling up to me.

MUM   You better shift if you really want to go in today! 5

STREET VOICE 2   The sound of the birds singing in the back garden.

STREET VOICE 3   Radio on. Music, news and travel.

NARRATIVE MARTIN   Dad drinking his tea too fast.

DAD	Oh, blimey, that's hot!

10

NARRATIVE MARTIN	He always does that.
DAD	Listen, love, do you think I should drive him in?
STREET VOICE 4	The chime of spoon on breakfast bowl.
MUM	I'd prefer it if you did, but I don't think he'll let you.

15

STREET VOICE 5	Post falling through the front door.
NARRATIVE MARTIN	Dogs barking next door.
DAD	I'll ask.
STREET VOICE 6	Everything back to normal.

20

PRESENT MARTIN	*(entering)* Don't even ask Dad, but thanks. I normally walk. I can walk today. Anyway Nat and the guys are coming soon. I'll be okay with them.

Doorbell rings. Natalie, Matthew and Mark enter.

ALL STREET VOICES	Just like normal.

25

NARRATIVE MARTIN	The world didn't stop when I got burned.
PRESENT MARTIN	Here we go.
NARRATIVE MARTIN	At first, on our side street, it was quiet, it was okay. I had time to get used to being back in the world. And things were cool. But then –

30

All actors fill the stage, creating a busy street.

– then it was the high street and it was people everywhere, faces from all directions, coming at me left, right and centre and I knew one thing for sure –

They all pause, stare.

– they were all looking at me. From buses,   35
from cars, from shops, from houses. I was
the centre of attention. And I wanted nothing
more than to run home with my coat on my
head. But this was a test. A test I'd set myself.
And I wasn't about to lose – not this early in   40
the race.

*The cast move again. School bell. They all become
pupils in a playground. Some are clearly looking
at Martin.*

MARK	Are you okay?
PRESENT MARTIN	I'd feel a bit easier if you all stopped asking me if I was okay. Okay?
MARK & MATTHEW	Okay. 45
PRESENT MARTIN	I'd just prefer it if we just talked about anything else, football, the weather, music – anything.

A pause.

MATTHEW	*(tentatively)* Nice weather – for the – time of year. 50

A beat, then they all laugh.

Well, you said!

School bell, the cast form a classroom.

FORM TUTOR	*(awkwardly)* Well, I must say it's good to see you all back. I hope everyone is looking forward to getting their teeth into the new term. I certainly am. It will be a challenging 55

one for us all, but let's hope the next few
months bring results for us all, eh? I know
that the holiday was a difficult time for – for
– some of you, but let's see if we can face
(pause, realises) let's, let's see if we can *look*   60
towards the coming term in a positive
manner, okay? Good. Right, off you go,
assembly!

*The class turns and is suddenly in assembly with
the Head Teacher in front of them.*

HEAD TEACHER   *(again, awkwardly)* New terms are, in a way,
new beginnings. New beginnings for us all.   65
This term should be a chance for us all to
put the past behind us and face the …
(pause, realises) embrace the future. And do
not forget that none of us succeeds without
the support of the rest of us. We all need   70
each other if this school, and all of you are
to reach your, and our potential. Thank you,
everyone. 4B lead off.

*The rest of the cast disperse, leaving Mark,
Present Martin and Matthew.*

PRESENT MARTIN   Did you ever get the feeling that someone
was talking *around* the subject, but not   75
actually talking *about* it?

MARK   They're doing their best.

MATTHEW   They're just trying to be nice.

PRESENT MARTIN   It'll be nicer when they don't have to try.

NARRATIVE MARTIN   And the day played itself out – not too easy,   80
but nothing I couldn't handle. I kept

thinking about what Anthony said, that the problem was with *them*, not with *me*.

NATALIE	You survived, then? 85
PRESENT MARTIN	I might even come back tomorrow, you never know.
NATALIE	Everyone would understand if you didn't.
PRESENT MARTIN	I think it's what people expect, and that's why I won't do it. 90
VIKKI	*(shyly)* Excuse me.
PRESENT MARTIN	Hiya.
VIKKI	I know what happened, we all heard about it. And I thought, well, I thought perhaps I should – well, here you go. 95
PRESENT MARTIN	What's this?
VIKKI	Nothing much. *(she exits)*
PRESENT MARTIN	*(opening the envelope)* 'Get well soon'?! Get well soon! Oi. Listen you! I am well. I am not ill, okay, can you hear me?! 100
NATALIE	Calm down!
PRESENT MARTIN	*(still shouting)* I'm not ill!
NATALIE	Martin. People are staring.
PRESENT MARTIN	They've been staring all day – and they'll stare all tomorrow too, so you better get 105 used to it okay, because I have to, don't I? Don't I!?
NATALIE	She didn't mean any harm – you're going to have to learn to tell the difference, you know.
NARRATIVE MARTIN	Like I said before, I hate it when other 110 people are right. She didn't mean any harm,

and I was going to have to learn to tell the
difference. So, after that, the week played
itself out. And things got a little easier. I
began to become part of the background.   115
Yesterday's news. There were a few little
episodes, some good:

Present Martin approaches Vikki.

PRESENT MARTIN   Listen, about the other day –

VIKKI   Are you going to shout at me again?

PRESENT MARTIN   I understand why you did it, gave me the   120
card.

VIKKI   You do?

PRESENT MARTIN   And it was nice and all that, but I meant what
I said. I am well. It just came out all wrong.
But thanks for the thought.   125

VIKKI   That's okay.

PRESENT MARTIN   Good.

NARRATIVE MARTIN   Some … not so good.

Simon enters.

SIMON   Sir says we have to get into pairs to do this
experiment.   130

PRESENT MARTIN   Right?

SIMON   So I thought I'd work with you.

PRESENT MARTIN   Simon, you never work with me.

SIMON   But I don't mind.

PRESENT MARTIN   You don't mind what?   135

SIMON   I think some people don't like it, but it
doesn't bother me.

PRESENT MARTIN	What doesn't?
SIMON	That you look minging.
PRESENT MARTIN	Me? Minging!? What are you on!? 140
SIMON	I didn't say you were minging – I said you *look* minging.
NARRATIVE MARTIN	And then I punched him and it all went wrong and we ended up in the Head's office. But some of it was, well *almost funny* I 145 guess.

The Street Voices take up places at a dining table.

PRESENT MARTIN	*(sitting down at the table)* Alright?
STREET VOICES	Yeah. Alright. Hiya.
PRESENT MARTIN	*(joking)* I'm beginning to wonder about this food, I haven't touched it yet and I'm sure I 150 just saw it moving on the plate.
MARGARET	Very funny. Why did you sit here?
PRESENT MARTIN	Because it's a seat – and I know it might be still alive but I want to eat my dinner. This is the dining hall isn't it? What's your 155 problem?
MARGARET	You're my problem, you're putting me off my food.
PRESENT MARTIN	You put lots of people off their food with your smelly breath, but we've all got to eat to live. 160
MARGARET	Why don't you sit with your friends? They're used to you.
PRESENT MARTIN	Why don't you sit on your own?
MARGARET	I was here before you. Look, there's lots of empty seats. Why did you come to spoil my 165 dinner?

PRESENT MARTIN   I can sit anywhere I want. There aren't any
                  rules about where people sit as long as it's on
                  a chair with a table in front of it. So if you've
                  got a problem, go and get advice – I'm not   170
                  moving.

MARGARET   I was going anyway. I don't have to sit here
                  and let you talk to me like that.

PRESENT MARTIN   So go, and shut your mouth.

MARGARET   You shut yours.   175

NARRATIVE MARTIN I guess, at least she had the guts to mention
                  it. But apart from those little 'glitches', that
                  first week went well. And the next week too,
                  but there was something, something was
                  odd, with the gang of three, but especially   180
                  with Nat – it was different … different in a
                  way I couldn't even pin down, couldn't put
                  my finger on.

ANTHONY   *(walks through again, unnoticed)* Some girls
                  back off, they start saying things like 'let's   185
                  just be friends' or 'we're getting too serious'
                  and things like that, but we all know what
                  they mean.

                  Martin picks up his phone, calls Natalie.

NATALIE   Hello?

PRESENT MARTIN   Natalie, it's me.   190

NATALIE   I was just about to call you – how did you
                  know?

PRESENT MARTIN   Know…?

NATALIE   You don't normally call this early on a
                  Saturday morning – you're never awake this   195
                  early! What have you heard?

PRESENT MARTIN	I haven't heard anything.
NATALIE	I've had some good news about a modelling job.
PRESENT MARTIN	I'm glad, and actually, that's part of it, I didn't sleep well last night. And when I did I was dreaming of us. And I want you to know that I'm here waiting for you. Something's gone wrong recently and it's all been strange, but we can be all right again. Sort yourself out and then it will be like before.
NATALIE	Me? Sort myself out? Sort what out?
PRESENT MARTIN	I think you're going to be a success Nat – a model, an actress, a dancer, you can do it all. And I'll be so proud to be with you. Everyone thinks we suit each other. I miss you.
NATALIE	What do you mean you miss me? You saw me every day last week, and if you go to school again next week you'll see me every day as well.
PRESENT MARTIN	Yeah, we see each other but it's not like before. What's happened, have you forgotten? I'm your boyfriend, you're my girlfriend, we got it going on. I really miss spending time with you.
NATALIE	Stop it, Martin. You're a nice person and I want to be your friend, but just stop taking everything so seriously. Things are changing, people move on. You must have noticed. I didn't think I needed to spell it out. Things have just – *cooled*, haven't they?

Line numbers: 200, 205, 210, 215, 220, 225

PRESENT MARTIN	*I* haven't cooled.
NATALIE	Then it must be me, mustn't it?
PRESENT MARTIN	Hold on ... I'm a 'nice person'? Things are 230 'changing'? What's changing? Just tell me, do you still want to go out with me?
NATALIE	Martin, you don't even know what you want, the last thing you want to be thinking about now is going out with me. 235
PRESENT MARTIN	What, are you telling me what to think now?
NATALIE	Why are you ringing me, Martin?
PRESENT MARTIN	Because I still want to go out with you. What's up with you? If you don't like my face, just say so. 240
NATALIE	Look, I thought you were ringing because you'd heard that I got a big job, I mean really big: TV, posters, big stuff. I'm the face of a whole cosmetics campaign. I thought you might have heard. Martin, I was really 245 happy before.
PRESENT MARTIN	How would I have heard if you didn't call me about it? I didn't realise I was down the list of people to call, Nat, I thought I was at the top. 250
NATALIE	Everything's changed, Martin – everything. And if you were honest about it, you'd know that was true. *(pause)* I'm going now.
PRESENT MARTIN	Someone told me recently that you shouldn't judge a person by what they look like. 255
NATALIE	And someone told me that it was human nature, just human nature, pure and simple, and you can't change it.

PRESENT MARTIN	Maybe they were wrong.

| NATALIE | Maybe they weren't. Look, I'll see you in school on Monday. We'll talk then. But you know, things are different now. They just are. And anyway … maybe we were getting too serious. And I guess, well … I think that I just need some time… | 260

265 |

At this Present Martin simply turns off his phone, leaving Natalie staring blankly at hers.

| NARRATIVE MARTIN | Now, that was not really what I needed at that point. Took the wind out of me all right. I'd been really stupid, hadn't seen it. Simple as that. And it all went, kind of, grey. *(Present Martin sits in a melancholy manner)* Look at me. Outside it was lovely weather, but I had a sort of little winter going on inside. It was odd, because when that happened, when I was sitting there, I realised some things hurt more than my face. | 270

275 |

Scene 3

Present Martin still sits as Matthew enters, Mum walks on too.

MUM	I'm so glad you've come, Matthew.
MATTHEW	How is he?
MUM	Still the same – he's been like it for ages now. We don't know what to do to help him shake it off.	5
MATTHEW	He has been strange at school.
MUM	He's not like himself, not like the old Martin.

MATTHEW We'll see how it goes tonight – I'm only going to the Unity though.

MUM But that'll be nice for him. Ease him back 10
into the idea of going out again. The kids at the Unity are nice aren't they?

MATTHEW Nice enough. Anyway, we should go.

MUM Call me if anything goes wrong. *Anything*,
okay? 15

MATTHEW No problem. *(to Present Martin)* Come on.

Mum kisses Present Martin and he leaves with Matthew. The Street Voices take up positions at the club.

NARRATIVE MARTIN Now the Unity Club, you should understand this, is run by a priest – and that is just so wrong on so many levels. I mean, this is a place where some kids came with their 20
parents, this was a club where you could see children line dancing. I mean! Come on! But I guess Matthew was still spooked by what had happened after that night at the Bassment, so I went for him and he went 25
for me – that's what's friends do isn't it?

REVEREND SAM *(calling across the room)* Hello Matthew, so good to see you.

PRESENT MARTIN Oh my God.

NARRATIVE MARTIN – the Reverend Sam. 30

MATTHEW Hi.

REVEREND SAM And you must be Martin?

PRESENT MARTIN I guess I must be. And you must be Reverend Sam.

REVEREND SAM	I am indeed!	35
PRESENT MARTIN	Now how is it that you know about me? Do you recognise my face by any chance?	
REVEREND SAM	Like it or not, Martin, you are something of a local celebrity.	
PRESENT MARTIN	I guess.	40
REVEREND SAM	*(calling to a youth)* Dean, we can do without the staring, and you Brian. *(he goes over to talk to them)*	
PRESENT MARTIN	*(quietly)* Matthew, we have got to leave. I hate it here. Lying in a hospital bed is more exciting than this. Let's go.	45
MATTHEW	Come on, Martin. We've only just got here, let's not start all that again. Where else are we going to go?	
PRESENT MARTIN	Anywhere. I'd rather just walk the streets than stay here.	50
MATTHEW	At least I feel safe here.	
PRESENT MARTIN	*(starting to exit) Safe* sounds like *boring* to me.	
MATTHEW	*Safe* isn't so bad, Martin.	
PRESENT MARTIN	Oh no, here comes the servant of the lord again.	55
REVEREND SAM	Martin. Aren't you staying with us?	
PRESENT MARTIN	·No, I can't. I promised my parents I'd be home early tonight.	
REVEREND SAM	I understand. Well, it's good to see you. I've been seeing quite a lot of Matthew lately, haven't I Matthew?	60

MATTHEW	Yes.
REVEREND SAM	Matthew knows that he's welcome to come here anytime – so are you. Please 65 remember, Martin, that our doors are open to anyone regardless of age, race … or … disability. Everyone needs to belong.
PRESENT MARTIN	Excuse me?
REVEREND SAM	All I am saying, Martin – 70
PRESENT MARTIN	I don't want to hear what you're saying, Just for once, you listen. You may think you're perfect, you may think you know everything and that you're going to heaven and all that, but let me tell you something, I am not 75 disabled. And I do not 'belong' here.
REVEREND SAM	Now Martin, calm down, I didn't say you were disabled. I just said all are welcome regardless of race or…
PRESENT MARTIN	'Disability'. Exactly. Do you say that to every 80 person who walks though the door? I don't think so. Why are you quoting your equal opportunity stuff to me, that's what I'd like to know. *(mocking)* Believe me, I do not need your 'equality' and 'we take everyone, 85 no matter how black or broken or burned they are' speech!
REVEREND SAM	Calm down now, Martin, calm down.
PRESENT MARTIN	I am calm. *(almost surprised)* Actually, I am. So, let me explain something to you. 90 Anything I could do before, I can do now. There are some things I can do better now, like *spotting the patroniser*. I have the same

69

	abilities as I ever had – I just look different. If you can't understand that, even with your hotline to heaven, then you're mentally challenged – not me. Goodnight Reverend Sam. Matthew, we're going.	95
REVEREND SAM	You've got me all wrong –	
PRESENT MARTIN	Have I?	100
REVEREND SAM	I wasn't trying to –	
PRESENT MARTIN	Like I said – we're going. *(he leaves)*	
MATTHEW	*(awkwardly staring at Sam)* I … erm, I should – should probably – follow him…	

Matthew runs up to Martin, who is pacing in the street.

PRESENT MARTIN	I'm *not* going back in there!	105
MATTHEW	Martin, that was… *(trying to find the right word)*	
PRESENT MARTIN	And I am not apologising to that… *(trying to find the right word too)*	
MATTHEW	…amazing. It was amazing.	
PRESENT MARTIN	Really?	
MATTHEW	The way you just came out with all that. Just knew what to say, just like that. Very cool. I haven't seen anything like that – and when you started you sort of – came alive. Like the *old Martin*, like my friend.	110

Present Martin thinks for a moment.

PRESENT MARTIN	Yeah … yeah.	115
NARRATIVE MARTIN	*(strolls through as Present Martin is thinking)* That was a real 'light bulb over the head'	

moment. A real 'suddenly all this makes
sense' moment.

PRESENT MARTIN This is part of my role in life now, isn't it?
Yeah ... some people may think I've got   120
some disease that they can catch, or that the
way I look makes me disabled, or stupid. So I
have to tell the people to look beneath my
face and see me, the real me, don't I? I need
to think about this – this is deep. Maybe   125
you can't understand. I'm fighting
discrimination.

MATTHEW Discrimination?

PRESENT MARTIN Yeah, facial discrimination. This is war
against the facialist! 'No' to Facial   130
Discrimination! That's what I say. It's the last
discrimination that people are still allowed,
isn't it?

MATTHEW Is it?

PRESENT MARTIN You can't say anything bad or judge anyone   135
if they're black or Asian or gay or blind or
whatever – but this, *(points to his face)* this is
different somehow. People think it's okay to
judge me before they know me. It's just fear.
And Matthew – I won't have it! Come on –   140
I'm going home, coming?

They enter.

We're back – Mum, you okay? *(he sees the
paper)* Oh.

MUM *(reading from the paper)* 'Today in Snaresbrook
Coroner's Court the coroner, Mr Murray Cole   145

heard how in August, Graham Fisher, an unemployed 17-year-old, stole a Ford Escort from Katherine Road in East Ham and then, with passenger Peter Mosley, 18, picked up two younger boys on the Boleyn Estate. 150 They were later spotted travelling at 100 mph by a police patrol. The police gave chase at high speed resulting in a crash at the junction of Green Street and Barking Road. Mosley failed to regain consciousness after 155 the crash and was pronounced dead three days later. Martin Turner, 15, was so badly burnt that he was hospitalised and had to undergo plastic surgery. The coroner heard that Turner and friend Mark Thorpe were 160 unaware that the car was stolen and believed they were receiving a lift home, but Fisher, who was also known as Apache, took them on a high-speed drive through Newham and Essex. On the day of the fatal crash Fisher 165 had consumed a large amount of heroin. Both he and Mosley were prominent members of a gang known as The Raiders Posse, well known to police for their criminal activities. The coroner heard that various 170 other members of the gang have since been arrested and charged with drug and firearms offences, but Thorpe and Turner, who is now out of hospital, only received a police caution due to their age and because they were 175 unwittingly involved in the crime. There were no members of Graham Fisher's family

at the hearing. The coroner recorded a
verdict of death by misadventure.'

They freeze.

NARRATIVE MARTIN   'Death by misadventure'? It should have   180
                    said 'murder'.

Scene 4

*The cast and Street Voices become pupils in the
playground.*

GYM TEACHER   Turner, Turner.

PRESENT MARTIN   Yes?

GYM TEACHER   I've been looking for you Turner. I want to
               ask you something.

PRESENT MARTIN   Me? I haven't done anything – and if Simon   5
                  says that I hit him again, that's a lie –

GYM TEACHER   I have been asked to put a gymnastics team
               together for the local competition at
               Newham Leisure Centre, so I need to ask
               you two favours.   10

PRESENT MARTIN   Me?

GYM TEACHER   Yes, you.

PRESENT MARTIN   What favours?

GYM TEACHER   A) I want you to be in the team.

PRESENT MARTIN   Oh yes, I can do that, I'll do some moves,   15
                  I'm still in good shape, and I can prepare a
                  bit too. Thanks.

GYM TEACHER   And B) I want you to be the captain of the
               team.

PRESENT MARTIN   What, me? You're joking, why me?   20

73

GYM TEACHER	Because you, Mr Turner, happen to be the best gymnast we have in the school – because you, Mr Turner, have some leadership qualities and because you, Mr Turner, have earned it.

25

PRESENT MARTIN	Me, are you serious, me? Honest?
GYM TEACHER	Yes, you, I'm serious, honest.

Present Martin goes from excited to unsure.

PRESENT MARTIN	I don't know. I don't mind being in the team, but captain? Me? I don't know if I'm up to it.
GYM TEACHER	I think you're up to it, and everybody else does.

30

PRESENT MARTIN	Is this for real? You're not just being nice – because…?
GYM TEACHER	This is for very real. And you know it's not my style to be nice because of, shall we say it, your face. I don't care what you look like – I care that you can help our school win. You can make me look good – honest enough for you?

35

PRESENT MARTIN	Yeah. Thanks.

40

GYM TEACHER	Deal?
PRESENT MARTIN	Okay, it's a deal. Shake on it.
NARRATIVE MARTIN	At first I thought this was just people being extra nice to me again, but apparently it was genuine, the rest of the team wanted something different and I do *different* better than any of them. Anyway, before the old captain left school I was the vice captain, so it shouldn't have been that much of a

45

surprise. I thought that they just wouldn't   50
want me to be the face of the team. That
evening I walked home with, what do they
say, 'a spring in my step' – but not for long. It
seems so stupid now, they were just kids,
probably no more than ten years old.   55

Scene 5

STREET VOICES	*(randomly calling, approaching and retreating)*

Ugly man.
You're the bad man.
Dog face.
Don't let him touch you, he'll kill you.
If you look at him for long you'll go blind.   5
Hey, throw twigs at him.
Freak-show boy.
Here's your dinner.
Get away, bogey man.
You haven't got no mum or dad.   10

Slowly, from the random words, a chant emerges.

Freak-show boy – freak-show boy – freak-
show boy!

PRESENT MARTIN	Go away, will you?
STREET VOICES	Freak-show boy – freak-show boy – freak-show boy! 15
PRESENT MARTIN	Leave me alone! *(he approaches but they evade him)*
STREET VOICES	Run! He's coming! *(they run off)*
PRESENT MARTIN	*(loudly out to the evening)* Leave me alone! *(quieter, downcast)* Leave me alone… *(he sits on a bench and puts his head in his hands)*

Narrative Martin sits on the bench too.

NARRATIVE MARTIN I couldn't believe it, it was the worst I'd felt   20
for ages. After all that I'd survived on the
streets and at school, it took a group of ten-
year-olds to send me to an all-time low. I
didn't know how to argue with kids of that
age. They seemed to hate me, like they   25
thought I was evil or something. It was so …
cruel. Eventually I felt like if I didn't get
myself up there and then I'd just lie there
and stay the night, with just self pity to keep
me covered. A part of me didn't care if I   30
stayed there forever. But most of me knew I
had to move.

*Narrative Martin physically pulls his other self up,
straightens him up.*

The one thing that got me moving was
thinking 'it can't get worse – it can't get
worse.'   35

Present Martin starts to walk off.

But what is it they say about adding insult to
injury…? I'd only got as far as East Ham Station.

*Natalie and a Young Man are cuddling, Natalie's
back to Present Martin.*

PRESENT MARTIN Oh no.

YOUNG MAN What are you staring at?

NATALIE *(looking at the guy)* What's up?   40

YOUNG MAN *(speaking as if Martin is stupid)* What – are –
you – staring – at?!

NATALIE *(turning to see him)* Oh…

YOUNG MAN Freak!

Present Martin simply walks off.

Scene 6

NARRATIVE MARTIN Bad time. Low point. If I was doing GCSE
Misery, I'd have been fine. I think I might
even have been able to cope with A-Level
Despair. Three days I was like that. Three
days I didn't go to school. Three days   5
I barely moved out of my room. Three days
listening to Dad and Mum trying to tempt
me to come out. Told me that if I stayed off
school I might miss out on being the captain
of the team. I didn't budge.   10

*We see Mum take Present Martin centre stage
where he is joined by Dr Owens, who is examining
his face. Mum waits some distance off.*

Eventually they made me an appointment at
the hospital – they claimed that they just
thought the Doc should look at the old face.
But I wasn't fooled. It was funny to be back
there.   15

*Dr Owens backs off a little, as if finishing the
examination.*

DR OWENS I'd say, in my professional, medical opinion,
that your injuries are healing up rather well. I
know they aren't as good as you'd hoped,
probably never will be, but I think you're
doing well – on the surface. But we're not all 20

'surface' are we? *(silence from Martin)* What's up, Martin? I should tell you, whatever it is, you can get over it. Life is going to do this to you, it will put hurdles in your way but you can get over them. Let me ask you a question. How do you feel about yourself? *(silence)* Nothing to say? Okay, off you go and I'll see you again in a few months. 25

Present Martin gets up and is about to leave, then turns.

PRESENT MARTIN   I was feeling okay.

DR OWENS   Good…? 30

PRESENT MARTIN   I got to the point where I felt all right – felt good. Back on the game, you know?

DR OWENS   So what's changed?

PRESENT MARTIN   I knew the deal, most people would be trying to be nice to me because they felt 35 sorry for me and that's okay, I understand that, but really small kids, they're supposed to be more honest, aren't they? They don't lie, they just tell the truth, and now I know how people really see me and I don't like it and I 40 don't like me.

DR OWENS   Okay, so what happened?

PRESENT MARTIN   I was in the park and all these kids started to call me names, not just a couple of them, there were loads of them. For no reason at 45 all, I mean if I'd said something to them that would be different but I didn't say a word. I don't care about anything now, I don't care about gymnastics, school or anything.

DR OWENS	Look, Martin, we know that when adults or even teenagers react badly to you it has more to do with their problems and hang-ups. Children of that age are different. Some of their reactions come from their parents telling them that anyone with a face that is different from theirs is a horrible person. Some children on the other hand think that someone who looks different is someone to laugh at, someone to insult. Some children even run from Father Christmas. And clowns – lots of children don't like clowns.	50
		55
		60
PRESENT MARTIN	I hate clowns. Anyway, what am I supposed to do in that situation? What would you do?	
DR OWENS	I'm afraid there is no textbook way of dealing with kids of that age, they are too unpredictable. Sometimes saying anything just makes it worse. You must realise that this type of thing is likely to happen again. Just be aware: all you can do is learn how to cope with it. You did well.	65
		70
PRESENT MARTIN	There's something else I need to tell you. Something that's been getting me really down.	
DR OWENS	What is it?	
PRESENT MARTIN	It's a girl thing.	75
DR OWENS	Oh, one of those, I know about those.	
PRESENT MARTIN	Forget it, it's nothing.	
DR OWENS	Hey…?	
PRESENT MARTIN	No, it's alright.	
DR OWENS	It's not is it?	80

PRESENT MARTIN	Sometimes I just feel *(clenching his fists)* angry.
DR OWENS	So do I, Martin, the world's not fair but if I hit people every time I got angry, my knuckles would hurt. There is another issue, something which needs to be sorted, and only you can do it. 85
PRESENT MARTIN	What, me?
DR OWENS	Yes, you. You see Martin, there's this gymnastics team and they really need someone who's got the talent to captain them. 90
PRESENT MARTIN	*(baffled)* Eh?
DR OWENS	Your mum told me. Your team doesn't need any upstarts or novices, they only want the best. Do you think you can help them out? 95
PRESENT MARTIN	I'll see what I can do. I really don't want to let the team down, we were doing some good work, we were.
DR OWENS	Well, they need you. I don't know if you know this, but you can always contact someone 100 here if you need to talk. We're not friends, we're not family, but sometimes it's easier to talk to someone like that. We have counsellors if you want to chat about anything, anytime. 105
PRESENT MARTIN	Thanks. But, I think … I'm cool.
DR OWENS	Good. Cool is good. See you later. Go face the world.

Present Martin steps outside, straight into Anthony.

ANTHONY	Martin. What's up, man? What you doing here? 110
PRESENT MARTIN	Alright, this is my mum, we're waiting for a cab.
MUM	Hello.
ANTHONY	I'm Anthony. Hiya.
MUM	Oh, *you're* Anthony. Martin has mentioned 115 you – you made quite an impression.
PRESENT MARTIN	Mum!? Embarrassing…
MUM	Sorry. *(she stands aside)*
PRESENT MARTIN	Hey, man, what are you up to?
ANTHONY	I came to see my doctor. I've got another 120 operation soon so they need to keep an eye on me.
PRESENT MARTIN	How did you get here? *(looking around)* Where's your parents?
ANTHONY	My parents? I don't know, they've probably 125 gone to some exhibition somewhere. That's all they do, go to art exhibitions. I came by bus as usual.
PRESENT MARTIN	You … travel by bus?
ANTHONY	All the time, no biggie. Should it be? 130 *(silence)* So, how's the lovely Natalie?
PRESENT MARTIN	I've finished with her, man. She's the past.
ANTHONY	Well, I did say that she wasn't bad. That could also mean she's not good. You see Martin, she may have been just too pretty. 135 Now don't get me wrong, I got nothing against pretty girls, some of my best girls are pretty girls, but sometimes they can get too

big for their boots. I like girls that have had a
few fights, you know, girls that are a bit   140
rough round the edges. My girlfriends have
to have a few scars, it gives them a bit of
character, if you know what I mean?

PRESENT MARTIN   Anthony, you're mad. But 'good-mad'.

ANTHONY   I wouldn't worry about her, guy, there's   145
plenty more fish in the sea – or dolphins in
the ocean, you get me?

PRESENT MARTIN   You're right, man – I'm moving on. She
thinks she's the queen or something.

ANTHONY   So now that you've been released from   150
Newham Parkside on good behaviour, what
are you up to?

PRESENT MARTIN   I'm the captain of my school gymnastics
team. We've got a friendly competition on
Saturday at Newham Leisure Centre. Come   155
down if you like.

ANTHONY   What, do you mean you're going to fly guy?

PRESENT MARTIN   Absolutely. I got hip-hops in my flick-flacks
and funky things in my Arab springs. I'm
gonna fly guy, but I'm gonna fly to some   160
heavy beats.

ANTHONY   Sounds good to me, guy. I'll be there – trust
me.

PRESENT MARTIN   *(quite seriously)* I do.

MUM   *(after a moment)* Come on you – bye   165
Anthony, very nice to meet you.

PRESENT MARTIN   *(watching Anthony leave)* Oh yeah … Mum,
where's Kansas?

Scene 7

The Street Voices are warming up as if they are the gym team.

NARRATIVE MARTIN I didn't go to school that Friday. What I did
was, I waited till school was over and then I
went to the squad practice. When I turned
up at the school gymnasium the squad were
gathered standing around Hewitt receiving   5
words of wisdom. I really don't think that
they were expecting me, well I didn't tell any
of them that I was coming. I think they were
planning life without me, and then when
they saw me everyone had something to say. 10

STREET VOICES Look who it is.

The prodigal acrobat.

Hey Martin, how are you doing?

Hey guy, we thought you had gone to
another team.   15

Aren't we good enough for you?

What are you doing tomorrow, mate?

Would you like to be our captain, mate?

If you're not too busy, that is.

GYM TEACHER Enough, you lot. Right then, welcome back.   20
Good to see you … eventually. We don't
have much time. Warm up, Martin. We'll go
through the exercises and when we've done
the compulsory stuff, you can do your
freestyle routine in your own time.   25

NARRATIVE MARTIN The practice session was a good one. It
didn't take me long to get back into the

swing of things and realise how much I had
meant to the team. They were really good to
me, not one of them made any negative   30
comments or complaints about the days I'd
missed; their big concern was getting ready
for the next day. At the end of the session
Hewitt gave us all brand-new kit: t-shirts and
tracky bottoms, they were sky blue with a   35
large white E logo on the back, for
Eastmorelands School. Kind of flashy. Kind
of cool.

GYM TEACHER Here, you lot, grab hold of these.

The team walk in and collect their kit.

PRESENT MARTIN Not sure about this! I don't normally let old   40
folk choose what I wear.

GYM TEACHER Watch it, Turner! I had to fight hard for
these. Look after them, they cost half of my
annual budget.

PRESENT MARTIN Joke! No, really … thanks. We appreciate it.   45
And – look – I've got something to say. I'm
sorry for missing this week's training and
thanks for bearing with me. I know I can be
difficult, but I don't mean to be. This
competition means a lot to me and I – I –   50
Well, I just want to say 'thanks', and that I
think that we can go all the way tomorrow,
yeah, we can do it. I know it, that's all I've
got to say.

Scene 8

STREET VOICE 1 Competition morning after night of fitful sleep. Bright and crisp.

STREET VOICE 2 Expectation in the air.

STREET VOICE 3 A covering of mist in the fields behind the leisure centre.   5

STREET VOICE 4 But inside, warm and noisy, bustle, gymnasts, coaches, teachers, bags and towels and people limbering up in a thousand different shapes.

STREET VOICE 5 Lady Mayoress speaking the speech she   10
speaks at every opening, every occasion. All competitors lining up, keeping moving, partly through nerves, partly through desire to keep muscles and tendons warm.

STREET VOICE 6 All eyes scanning the four hundred   15
spectators.

STREET VOICE 1 Where's my mum? Where's Gran?

STREET VOICE 2 Where's my boyfriend?

Present Martin is scanning the crowd.

NARRATIVE MARTIN I couldn't see *anyone* I knew. Not a soul. I suddenly felt alone, unsupported and   20
downhearted. But then…

MARCIA *(calling and waving)* Martin!

NARRATIVE MARTIN I looked up but couldn't see who it was.

MARCIA Martin! Over here.

NARRATIVE MARTIN Marcia – the girl from the Bassment? Weird.   25
Quite what she was doing there was beyond me – I barely knew her.

MARCIA	Hiya – good luck!
NARRATIVE MARTIN	Clearly my moves on that night impressed her or something. Or maybe she was friends with someone from another school – who knows.
VIKKI	Give it all you've got!
NARRATIVE MARTIN	The girl who gave me the card – I didn't even know her name. Surely she wasn't there for me?!
VIKKI	You show them your best moves, Martin!
ANTHONY	Fly like an eagle – skinny white boy.
NARRATIVE MARTIN	Anthony *(looks closer)* standing with Mark and Matthew... *(nods to them)*.
ANTHONY	Wipe the floor with the opposition. No mercy!
NARRATIVE MARTIN	'No mercy,' it was weird hearing that again. And just before it all started – I saw her.

Everything else is still and quiet as Martin watches Natalie come in and take her seat.

What was that all about? Friendship, support, an apology, some attempt to get back together – who knows? And I, for one, didn't have time to work it out.

ANNOUNCER	Ladies and gentlemen, boys and girls, settle down please, the games are about to begin. The judges will assess each competitor's poise, balance, co-ordination, elegance, confidence in execution and correctness. At the end of the competition, the points will be totalled. The freestyle competition will be judged separately.

30

35

40

45

50

55

NARRATIVE MARTIN	The first event was the trampolines, nice to watch, nice not to be first up … but then I was on. When I walked out I became so conscious of my face. I knew that every person in the hall was looking at me. I was 60 tempted to look around to see how they were looking, I mean were they looking at a gymnast or a face? I tried not to show my nervousness, I just looked straight ahead of me, trying hard not to lose my concentration. 65
ANNOUNCER	And now on the floor, representing Eastmorelands, Martin Turner.
VIKKI	Go on Martin, you can do it.
MARCIA	Show 'em, Martin.
MATTHEW	Do it. 70
MARK	Come on, Martin.
MUM	You're alright, son.
ANTHONY	Be cool and deadly, fly guy.
ANNOUNCER	Quiet, please.
NARRATIVE MARTIN	Unless you've ever felt it I don't know if 75 you'll know what I'm saying, but standing there, feet on that mat, that was when I got that feeling – transformed – transported.
STREET VOICES	*(whispering, off)* Like no one is watching.
NARRATIVE MARTIN	From the first move I forgot about my face, 80 the judges, Nat, the whole room.
STREET VOICES	*(whispering, off)* Like no one is watching.
NARRATIVE MARTIN	It was just me, the mat and gravity.

Still images, like at the Bassment.

Two steps, turning jump, smooth landing,
two hand springs and front tucked   85
somersault. Nice. Cartwheel, cartwheel, three
Arab springs, four flick-flacks. All spot on.
You know when it's right.

Get to the far corner, change direction, fast
as a cat, smooth as water, I could hear that   90
the crowd, not one of them was breathing,
not yet. Two headsprings, a forward roll,
another two Arab springs and four more
flick-flacks ending with a back somersault.
Perfect landing. Solid, stable, smooth. And   95
the audience breathed.

Applause and cheers from the crowd.

DAD   Well done, son.

ANTHONY   Nice one, Martin.

GYM TEACHER   Well done, Martin.

Over the past few lines, a chant begins.

CROWD   Martin, Martin, Martin, Martin, Martin,   100
Martin, Martin.

ANTHONY   You see that man there? He is the man, he is
the brother, you can't beat him.

NARRATIVE MARTIN   We sat back and we watched the rest of the
teams do their stuff. They all did the   105
various disciplines, some individual stuff,
some pairs, some big groups. And we sat
knowing our best card was about to be played.

ANNOUNCER   And now we come to the freestyle section.

NARRATIVE MARTIN   It was freestyle; we could walk away with   110
it – no problem.

ANNOUNCER   Each team will use all members on the floor,
             demonstrating their range and skill.

NARRATIVE MARTIN   Man, you should have seen them. Some were
             … accurate, but anyone can be accurate.   115
             Even gymnastics needs some soul, some
             heart. So we sat through some ballet-
             flavoured mush and some classical-style stuff.
             Then we were up! I figured all the judges
             needed to see was an inspired   120
             performance, and we were up for that.

             The team gathers with a hip-hop attitude.

             We waited for silence – absolute silence.

             *A loud, heavy beat comes crashing in. Narrative
             Martin has to call over the noise.*

             If ever a mat was rocked, it was that day.
             Someone should have been there to take
             photographs, someone should have   125
             documented it, recorded it for posterity. It
             was so sweet!

             *Music comes in. The team presents still images in
             rhythm.*

             Start with a semi-circle, each of us for a few
             seconds in the centre, giving it our all.
             Moonwalk back to the edge, perfectly in   130
             time, perfectly in step. Split off into pairs,
             forward somersault, backwards too, bang on
             the beat, right on the mark. Half down in the
             splits, half up in the air, then swap. Under
             the legs, over the back, too much for the   135
             audience to see, and they were clapping and

cheering, going for it big-time. Then bang, bang, bang – windmills, pretzel, six step, air-chair, back-spin. All to the edge of the mat, cheesy disco hitchhike dance, just for the 140 laugh, a bit of cheek. Transported. Transformed. Then old-school body-popping, robot, into something like Kung-Fu mixed with Cossack. Run to the edge, all turn like a school of fish in the sea or birds on the 145 wing, and run in and somersault, and stop – BAM! Muscle-man pose!

Stillness on the final pose, huge applause. The music stops and the team run off, pleased with themselves.

ANNOUNCER Ladies and gentlemen, boys and girls. I want to take this opportunity to thank all eight schools for taking part in this competition. 150 The results are in! And so it now gives me great pleasure to announce the winners of the first Newham's Gymnastics Friendlies. In third place we have Eastmorelands.

Applause.

GYM TEACHER Well done everyone, you did well. 155

PRESENT MARTIN *(to the team)* Yeah, well done – but we still got the freestyle winners to be announced, so watch this space.

ANNOUNCER In second place, we have Saint Katherine's.

Applause.

And I am delighted to announce that in first 160 place we have Compton Park.

Applause.

And now, as you know we had a separate
competition for freestyle.

PRESENT MARTIN Here we go.

ANNOUNCER And this special prize goes to the team   165
that impressed the judges with the most
original display of gymnastics.

PRESENT MARTIN This is almost unfair … too easy.

ANNOUNCER Unfortunately there is some bad news.
Eastmorelands have, sadly, been   170
disqualified from this part of the
competition.

Sighs and boos, calls of 'no' and 'unfair'.

PRESENT MARTIN What?

GYM TEACHER Stay calm, Martin.

ANNOUNCER The judges have declared that the   175
Eastmorelands display was a performance of
pop music dance, and not a display of the art
of gymnastics.

PRESENT MARTIN *What?!*

More calls from the team and crowd.

ANNOUNCER So, it gives me great pleasure to announce   180
that the winner of the freestyle competition
is Kirton High. *(exits)*

Polite applause.

PRESENT MARTIN *(to Gym Teacher)* They were crap, listen to
those people, everyone knows they were crap.

| GYM TEACHER | Calm down, Martin, you may not like the judges' decision but that's no way to talk about your fellow competitors. | 185 |

PRESENT MARTIN But we were the best, everyone knows that. We rocked the people, we got them moving. It's *obvious* that we were the most original. 190

GYM TEACHER You have to respect the judges' decision, that's part of the sport, Martin. I know you were good, you know you were good, that's good enough.

PRESENT MARTIN Can't we do something? Can't we make a complaint? 195

GYM TEACHER Calm down, Martin, no one's ever changed a judge's decision by complaining.

PRESENT MARTIN But we were the best!

GYM TEACHER Not the best at pleasing the judges, and that is what the whole thing is about! It's what you're meant to do – we didn't do it – end of story. 200

PRESENT MARTIN *(to the team)* I'm sorry, it's my fault. Maybe I should have worked out something a bit more *normal*. I made us do all that work just to get disqualified. 205

ANTHONY *(approaching, angry)* Hey, man. Who's Kirton High? I saw better gymnastics in hospital.

PRESENT MARTIN Anthony, man, did you see what they done to us? It's not fair, man. 210

ANTHONY Martin, believe me guy, them judges need to be born again. They got no taste, no eyes, no ears and certainly no rhythm.

| MARCIA | Martin, you still got the moves, give me a hug. | 215 |

Hugs him.

| NARRATIVE MARTIN | Now *that*, I couldn't believe. |

| PRESENT MARTIN | Thanks … Marcia. |

| MARCIA | Well done. |

| NARRATIVE MARTIN | I was just pleased I remembered her name! | 220 |

Marcia kisses him on the cheek.

| MARCIA | You and your bodily functions, wicked and wild. |

| VIKKI | *(approaching)* You were so good, Martin – all of you – congratulations. |

She kisses him. A quiet moment as Marcia and Vikki size each other up, then Natalie approaches – is about to say something but thinks better of it. She leaves, watched by the other girls.

| NARRATIVE MARTIN | *(pointing to the scene)* And that is *exactly* how it happened – honest! | 225 |

| PHOTOGRAPHER | *(approaching the Gym Teacher)* Excuse me. You're in charge, are you? |

| GYM TEACHER | I am. |

| PHOTOGRAPHER | Any chance of a photo of the team now? | 230 |

A silence descends.

| GYM TEACHER | A photo? Why not. They've done our school proud. |

| PRESENT MARTIN | Photo – you didn't say anything to me about a photo. |

GYM TEACHER	It's not unusual for photos to be taken, 235 Martin. You know that. You know the form. This is just business as usual. We can treat today as different if you want…?
PRESENT MARTIN	I – I just thought that –
GYM TEACHER	If it's a problem we can just *(is about to say* 240 *'say no photographs')*.
PRESENT MARTIN	It's not a problem. It's not.
GYM TEACHER	You sure? You *are* the boss.
PRESENT MARTIN	Sure.
PHOTOGRAPHER	Great, we'll do it here if that's okay.

Photos of the team.

PHOTOGRAPHER	Very good. That's fine. 245

Martin's parents walk up.

MUM	I'm so proud of you Martin – you did good.
PRESENT MARTIN	Thanks, Mum.
DAD	Are you okay, son?
PRESENT MARTIN	*(almost baffled that he is)* Actually, Dad – yeah, I am. 250
DAD	Good. We'll wait for you outside. *(they exit)*
ANTHONY	*(still really angry)* You should have won that. Don't you feel bad? Don't you feel cheated?
PRESENT MARTIN	Anthony, man, I have to tell you, I do feel cheated but deep down I don't feel so bad. 255
ANTHONY	I would, man, I'd be angry. I'd be making lots of noise if I were you.
PRESENT MARTIN	Well, I feel sorry for my team, but I don't feel sorry for myself.

It's not the winning that matters, or even 260
the taking part. For me, it's just the being
here. The truth is, Anthony, that today, I am
the winner.

*Team, Martin, Anthony & co clear the stage. Street
Voices take up positions as at the start.*

Epilogue

STREET VOICES
1, 2 & 3
This was a street story. Urban, capital,
Eastside. No green fields, no cattle grazing,
just trees in parks with benches and bins.

STREET VOICES
4, 5 & 6
This was a story of grey cracked paving slabs
and charcoal tarmac. Seasons of winter pale- 5
slate skies and summer sun heat-haze on
burn-black tacky tar.

NARRATIVE MARTIN
It was a time like no other, something was
lost, something was found. I changed –
inside and out. I grew. Yeah … this was the 10
story of how I went from the gang of three –
to the gang of me.

Narrative Martin is left alone onstage.

NARRATIVE MARTIN
You have to look beyond the face
To see the person true,
Deep down within my inner space 15
I am the same as you;
I've counted since that fire burnt
The many lessons I have learnt.

Past Martin joins him.

PAST MARTIN
You have to talk to me and not
The skin that holds me in, 20

I took the wisdom that I got
To make sure that I win:
I've counted weaker folk than me
Who look but truly cannot see.

Present Martin joins them.

PRESENT MARTIN   I've seen compassion from the blind   25
                   Who think with open eyes,
                   It's those that judge me quick you'll find
                   Are those that are unwise:
                   Why judge the face that I have on,
                   Just value my opinion.   30

NARRATIVE MARTIN   Friends will come and friends will go.
                   Now I need friends that feel,

PAST MARTIN   My friends have changed so much and now
                   I make sure they are real:

NARRATIVE MARTIN   I took the ride and paid the price,   35
                   I can't afford to do that twice.

PAST MARTIN   I came to here from ignorance,
                   I cannot call it bliss.

PRESENT MARTIN   And now I know the importance
                   Of loving me like this: 40

NARRATIVE MARTIN   To leave behind that backward state
                   Of judging looks is very great.

PRESENT MARTIN   I'm beautiful, I'm beautiful.

NARRATIVE MARTIN   This minor fact I know,

PAST MARTIN   I tell you it's incredible –   45
                   Near death has made me grow:
                   Look at me,

NARRATIVE MARTIN   Smile,

PRESENT MARTIN   You are now seeing

  ALL MARTINS   A great thing called a human being.   50

END

Notes on principal characters

The three Martins

All three of the 'Martins' will obviously share many character traits and mannerisms. In essence Martin is a likeable lad, cheeky, but with enough charm and wit to keep him personable. Terms like 'rough diamond' or 'loveable rogue' could have been coined for Martin.

Past Martin

Before the crash Martin is happy-go-lucky and pretty carefree. He is popular and living for the moment. Though we see him as a chancer and something of a trouble-maker, he retains a warmth which makes us like him. Past Martin really ceases to exist as he is laid on the hospital bed at the end of Act One.

Present Martin

After the crash we see Martin as confused and in physical and psychological pain. He takes time to get his bearings and focus again. In many areas of his life he finds that 'the old rules no longer apply', and it takes time to adjust to his new situation. We see this version of Martin grow and develop more than any other character.

Narrative Martin

This is Martin with the wisdom of the experience he has gone through. He has things in perspective and is undaunted by the future. He is a bright, positive presence on the stage. He is perhaps something like the *resilient spirit of Martin*, made flesh.

Street Voices

The Street Voices are key to the successful telling of this tale; they set the tone of the piece, developing a fluid feeling to the play which can establish a place and a time very smoothly. They have a heightened way of speaking which sets them apart, but they can also slip in and out of taking parts in the scenes.

Mark

Something like Martin in his approach to life, but a little shorter on wit and charm. Mark probably wants to be a little more like Martin.

Matthew

Earnest and pretty risk-averse, Matthew tends to want to play it safe in life and sees problems arise where others just see fun.

Natalie

Natalie is probably too pretty for her own good. She's ambitious for herself and can appear to be shallow. She should not be played, however, as totally unfeeling for what she does to Martin. She too will be having feelings of a complex and contradictory nature.

Mum and Dad

In some ways, they are *all* Mums and Dads. She is bustling, effusive and very open with her emotions, he is more internalised and happy to talk about *things* rather than *feelings*. Though something of a cliché, I hope that there is a truth to them which readers and performers will recognise.

Anthony

A maverick who has learned over a long time the lessons that Martin is only now coming to terms with, Anthony demands that the world take him for what he is, not for what he looks like. Confident, upbeat and prepared to challenge the world head-on, we need to see that Martin has much to gain from Anthony's friendship.

ACTIVITIES

Activity 1: Past and present

This activity asks you to look over Act One and separate the scenes that take place in the past from those that take place in the present. You will then make a flow-diagram showing in order: (i) the main things that happen to Martin up to the crash, (ii) what happens to Martin in the hospital.

a Begin making a list of scenes that show past events. Briefly note down where they take place, like this:

- Scene 1: pages 8–9: at school just before the holidays
- Scene 2: on the street, the evening of the same day
- Scene 3: at the fair near Epping Forest, a few days later.

Add a short description of what happens during each of these scenes.

b Continue making your 'past events' list up to the end of Act One. Make a separate list of present events, all of which take place in the hospital.

c Now convert your two lists into a flow diagram to put on display. Use colours to highlight different characters or the different settings of past events. It could begin like this:

Past events	**Present events**
Martin in school looking forward to the holidays	Martin in hospital just after the crash – his parents arguing about who is to blame
Martin in the street looking for Natalie and planning his evening	Martin in hospital about to come round after the crash

Activity 2: Highs and lows

This activity asks you to look over Act Two and trace the ups and downs of Martin's attempt to live a normal life. You will then make a graph to show the high and low points he experiences.

a Draw the outline of a graph like this:

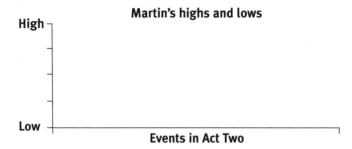

Decide when Martin is at his highest point:

- When he comes home from hospital?
- When he is made captain of the gym team?
- When Marcia kisses him at the gym competition?

Decide when Martin is at his lowest point:

- When he is disqualified from the gym competition?
- After his phone call to Natalie?
- When the children call him 'freak-show boy'?

Plot these highest and lowest points on the graph. Devise a Key to:

- show the events these points represent
- explain **why** the events make Martin feel high or low.

b Plot six to ten events on your graph; decide where they fit on the scale of 'high' to 'low', then make a clear and attractive copy of your chart to put on display.

Activity 3: Past Martin's character

This activity asks you to describe the character of Past Martin – to show what Martin is like before the crash.

a Read the dialogue between Past Martin, Mark, Matthew and their Form Tutor in Act One Scene 1 (pages 8–9). Then copy and complete the chart below to show how Martin is presented in this scene. One entry has been made for you; add **two** more.

Past Martin's character	Evidence in the form of a quotation
Very sure of himself	'I learned a lot in those sex lessons! I'll use that this holiday'

b Compare the points on your chart with a partner's. Then read the extracts listed below:

- Act One Scene 2: pages 12–14
- Act One Scene 4: pages 16–20
- Act One Scene 8: pages 25–29.

In these extracts. Does Past Martin seem:

- likeable
- self-centred
- hot-headed
- lacking confidence?

Add **three** further points to your chart. These need not be the same as other people's.

c Read the comments about Past Martin on page 98: 'happy-go-lucky and pretty carefree … living for the moment … something of a trouble-maker … he retains a warmth that makes us like him'.

Use these comments and your chart to write a character profile of Past Martin. It should be three paragraphs long and should use the P(Point), E(Evidence), E(Explanation) method.

Activity 4: What part do the Street Voices play?

This activity asks you to imagine you are in charge of producing the play. You will read three extracts that make use of the Street Voices, then decide how you would present them on stage.

a Read the extracts listed below:

- Act One Scene 4: pages 16–20
- Act One Scene 6: pages 22–24
- Act One Scene 12: pages 37–42.

Then discuss:

- the Street Voices' different functions, e.g: telling parts of the story, acting the roles of unnamed characters, creating the right atmosphere
- why the Street Voices are important to the staging of the play (refer to the 'Notes on principal characters' on page 98 *(sharply, indignantly)*).

b In groups, plan, rehearse and act out a performance of **one** of the extracts listed above, books in hands. Concentrate on:

- the positioning and movement on stage of the Street Voices
- how the Street Voices should sound
- how the Street Voices should interact with each other and with the named characters.

c As a class, discuss the group performances. Which ones do you think would make more of an impression on an audience? Why?

d Use the work you did in parts a, b and c to write Producer's notes on these three extracts. Include points about the costumes you would use for the Street Voices.

Activity 5: 'Dear Martin...', 'Dear Natalie...'

This activity asks you to trace the relationship between Martin and Natalie up to page 66 of the play. You will then write a letter from one to the other shortly after the crash.

a Read the following extracts, then fill in a copy of the chart below.

- Act One Scene 2: pages 12–14
- Act One Scene 6: pages 22–24.

Impressions of Natalie	Martin's feelings for Natalie	Natalie's feelings for Martin

(i) Why do Martin and Natalie have different views about the Bassment club?

(ii) What is Natalie's opinion of Martin as a gymnast?

b Now read these two extracts and add further points to your chart.

- Act One Scene 8: pages 25–29
- Act One Scene 12: pages 37–42.

(i) Why does Martin agree to go to the Bassment club?

(ii) Why does Natalie let Martin kiss her (page 44)?

c As a class, share your ideas from questions a and b, then read aloud Martin's phone call to Natalie in Act Two Scene 2 (pages 63–66). Add further points to your chart to show how Natalie and her feelings for Martin have changed.

d By yourself, imagine you are **either** Martin **or** Natalie at the end of the phone call. Write a letter to the other expressing your feelings about:

- their relationship in the past
- whether they should continue as boyfriend and girlfriend.

Activity 6: One play, three Martins

This activity asks you to examine the structure of Act One. You will then write a commentary, explaining why the playwrights chose this structure and saying how effective you think it is.

a   Read the Adaptor's notes (page 6) about the way Act One is built up. Then discuss:

- what he means by 'fairly fractured' and 'fluid'
- why he chose this narrative structure rather than 'a simple unfolding of chronological events'.

b   Look carefully at Act One Scenes 2 and 3 and Act One Scenes 6 and 7. Then fill in a copy of the chart below.

Scene	What the scene shows
Act One Scene 2	
Act One Scene 3	
Act One Scene 6	
Act One Scene 7	

c   Read Act One Scene 9 (pages 29–32), then discuss:

- why the playwrights include two different voices for Martin in this scene: Narrative Martin and Present Martin
- what effect this device is meant to have on the audience
- how you would present the two Martins on stage if you were producing the play.

d   Write a commentary on the structure of Act One using this title: Explain how Act One of *Face, the play* has an unusual structure and why it has been chosen. How effective do you think an audience will find it?

Activity 7: Telling Martin to his face

This activity asks you to look at how various characters react to Martin after his face has been burned in the crash. You will then take part in a class discussion about how they help or hinder Martin's attempt to live a normal life in Act Two Scenes 1–3.

a Look carefully at Martin's conversations with the Form Tutor and Natalie in Act Two Scene 1 (pages 53–56). Then copy and fill in the chart below.

Character	Do they help or hinder Martin? How? (1 = 'help him a lot', 5 = 'hinder him a lot')
Form Tutor	
Natalie	

b Read Act Two Scene 2 (pages 56–66), then add further entries to your chart to show how the following characters help or hinder Martin:

- the Head Teacher
- Vikki
- Simon
- Margaret.

c Look carefully at how Reverend Sam speaks to Martin in Act Two Scene 3 (pages 67–70). Then add a further entry to your chart.

d Now take part in a class debate about how much of a help or a hindrance to Martin these characters are. Focus on:

- what they say to Martin
- the way they say it
- how Martin reacts to each of them.

See if you can agree on a rank order for the characters, with the most helpful at the top and the least helpful at the bottom.

Activity 8: Anthony's influence on Martin

This activity asks you to explain how and why Anthony has a strong influence on Martin in the later part of the play. You will then write extracts from Martin's diary in which he describes his meetings with Anthony and how Anthony helps him cope with his disfigurement.

a Fill in a copy of the diagram below.

Anthony's influence on Martin's life

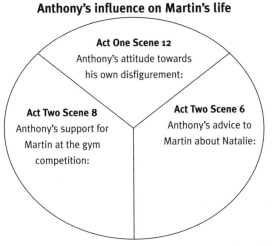

Act One Scene 12
Anthony's attitude towards his own disfigurement:

Act Two Scene 6
Anthony's advice to Martin about Natalie:

Act Two Scene 8
Anthony's support for Martin at the gym competition:

b As a class, compare the points on your diagram, then plan **three** entries Martin makes in his diary after each of the scenes in which Anthony appears. You should discuss:

- why Martin feels better about himself because of Anthony
- how Anthony helps Martin to cope with
  (i) prejudice
  (ii) disappointment
- why Anthony becomes a role model for Martin.

c Write several entries in Martin's diary that centre on Anthony and his influence. Base your style of writing on the speech style that Narrative Martin uses in the play.

Activity 9: A group improvisation

This activity asks you to take part in a drama improvisation. You will act out the inquest into Graham Fisher's death.

a Read the newspaper report of the inquest (pages 71–73). Then talk about what an inquest is and how it is conducted. Check the following factual details:

- why the crash occurred
- what happened to Graham Fisher and Peter Mosley
- what happened to Martin's friend Mark Thorpe
- why the coroner recorded a verdict of 'death by misadventure'.

b In groups, plan, rehearse and act out the inquest. You will need the following characters:

- Mr Murray Cole, the coroner
- the police officer driving the patrol car
- the police officer who interviews Martin in Act One Scene 13 (pages 42–51)
- Mark Thorpe
- Natalie.

The coroner will question each of the four witnesses in turn. They must tell the truth as it is shown to us in the play.

To prepare, the person playing the coroner should note down the questions s/he will ask each witness, and each witness should note down the answers they intend to give.

When you come to improvise this scene, make sure that you use formal language, to give a true impression of a legal hearing.

c As a class, review your improvisations. What did you find most difficult in acting out this scene? What advice would you give to other groups doing this activity in the future?

Activity 10: A newspaper report

This activity asks you to imagine you are a journalist on *The Newham Chronicle*. You will write a newspaper report about the gym competition at the end of the play.

a Read Act Two Scene 8 (pages 85–95). Then list the facts on which your newspaper report will be based, for example:

- who wins the team competition?
- who wins the freestyle part of the competition?
- why is Eastmorelands disqualified from the freestyle?
- how does the Eastmorelands gym teacher react to this?

b Now read a sports report from a local newspaper. Make notes about:

- *the headline:* how does it make a strong impression on the reader?
- *the first paragraph:* what information does it give?
- *the language:* how does the choice of language make the report sound dramatic?
- *interviews:* how are these worked into the report to help tell the story?
- *the presentational devices:* how do these add to the impact of the report?

c Use your notes from questions a and b above to write your report for *The Newham Chronicle*. Include interviews with **two** of the following:

- the organiser of the competition
- Anthony
- Martin's gym teacher
- Vikki.

If possible, produce your final version on a computer so that it looks like a real newspaper report. Make full use of presentational devices.

Activity 11: Publicising the play

This activity asks you to imagine that your school is putting on a production of *Face, the play*. You are part of the publicity team.

a Design and produce an advertising poster for your production. It will be displayed around the school and in your neighbourhood. It should include:

- a striking and appropriate image
- the names of the playwrights
- the dates and times of performances
- the location of performances.

b Plan and write a 75-word synopsis of the play. This will give an idea of the story – just enough to interest an audience without revealing everything that happens. Produce your final version on a computer in leaflet form.

c Look at some theatre programmes, then plan and produce a programme for your school's production of *Face, the play*.

Divide up the tasks. Your programme could include:

- a cast list: choose actors from your class or year
- a synopsis of scenes: show the order they come in and where they take place
- an interview with Benjamin Zephaniah about the play and the novel on which it is based: find information on the Internet
- a note from the producer about the reasons for choosing the play and the style of the production
- interviews with some of the actors about rehearsals and what they think of the characters they play.

Activity 12: Overcoming facial prejudice

This activity asks you to read the Epilogue, then annotate a copy of it to show how it sums up the play's main themes. You will use this to write your own considered response to *Face, the play*.

a Read the Epilogue (pages 95–97). Then take a copy of it and make notes showing how it refers back to events and characters at different points in the play, for example:

> You have to talk to me and not
> The skin that holds me in,　　**(1)**

> I took the wisdom that I got
> To make sure that I win　　**(2)**

> I've counted weaker folk than me
> Who look but truly cannot see.　　**(3)**

KEY: **(1)** Anthony and Dr Owen always talk to the 'inner Martin', not the boy with the scarred face
(2) Martin doesn't win the gym competition, but he wins the respect of everyone watching
(3) Applies to Reverend Sam, Simon and possibly Natalie

b As a class, share your ideas from question a. Then choose **four** points you have noted that you think express between them the play's moral or theme.

Put these onto the writing frame that your teacher will give you. Each one will introduce a separate paragraph.

c Use your writing frame to plan an essay with the title: 'My views on what the play shows about the problems of facial prejudice and how they can be overcome.' Write your essay using the PEE method.